THE BELOVED

JANNAT HUSSAIN

Made with ❤ on the Notion Press Platform
www.notionpress.com

Sugarplum, you're miraculous with all your issues, scars, strength and grace. I'm so damn proud of you.

Prologue

2 May 2003

How long can someone live in their delusions before they become suffocating?

How long before reality dissolves completely?

How long do I have to stare at walls—blink, blink, blink—

before they stop bleeding?

How much longer do I have to claw at the skin of my neck to stop the worms from coming out?

I press my palm against my neck and count under my breath. One... two... three... four... five... six... seven... eight.

They're not real.

They can't be real.

I watch my flesh tear apart it always starts small, a singular, cut then it, expands tearing my skin deeper and deeper till the worms comes pouring out.

They have always been there, crawling beneath my skin, in my veins. In my blood. The same blood that connects me to my daughter.

I run to my daughter's nursery, my heart pounding in my chest.

I look at her.

I must make sure.

Make sure she's okay.

Make sure she's still real.

I take in the ivory of her skin, the soft rise and fall of her small chest, her lashes fluttering in sleep. I blink once, twice—and suddenly, my hands, they're fine. The flesh is whole again.

The worms have gone back inside.

"They're from her," a voice whispers.

I freeze.

No.

No, they're not. They were there before she was born.

"Look under her skin," the voice insists.

"Look. You'll find out."

"Like mother, like daughter."

The voices close in, pressing against my skull.

"Did you tell your daughter you're rotting?"

"No." The word rips out of me in a scream. No.. no..NO.

I struggle to breathe, a chill running down my spine.

Samara stirs, startled by my voice, her small face crumpling. No, baby, don't cry. I reach for her, my trembling fingers brushing her cheek— but the moment my skin touches hers, it burns.

No. Skin doesn't burn like that. This isn't real.

"...One... two... three... four... five... six... seven... eight."

I pick her up, holding her against me.

My baby.

My miracle.

She looks up at me, and I see myself in her eyes. We share the same eyes.

The feeling from the first time I held her washes over me. I couldn't believe something so perfect, so beautiful, could come from me. My husband was so happy, he called her a blessing.

She is indeed a blessing in my life of sin. I touch her cheeks—they're so soft. She's small. So delicate.

I smile. As if sensing it, her tiny lips curve.

Samara.

I named her Samara before I even saw her. I never believed in God, but she became my faith.

 God will protect her. Because I... I don't think... I'll be able to.

"I love you so much," I whisper, pressing a kiss to her forehead.

"No, you don't," the voice mocks me.

"You'll kill her."

I flinch. My hands go cold.

Samara's eyes open, dripping with red.

No.

No, no, I blink—once, twice, three times—and she's fine.

She's fine.

But something—someone—is behind me.

I spin around.

Nothing.

My breaths are shallow as tears stream down my cheeks.

I set Samara down, tucking the surrounding blanket, and stumble back to my bedroom. The voices grow louder and louder until they are all I can hear.

Why is this happening?

I took the pills.

Didn't I?

"Your daughter isn't real," someone whispers in my ear.

I choke on air. No. I just saw her. I held her.

I did.

I Did.

Didn't I?

My hands fumble for the drawer, searching for the pills, but my reflection catches me off guard. I freeze.

My face is slick with tears, with a thread dangling from my pupil.

I reach up and pull. It unravels, tearing my eyes bit by bit, the thin flesh, slipping from my eye, pooling in my palm. Blood slithers down my cheek, splattering onto the floor. My eyes hurt.

I tug at my hair, a habit I learned to snap myself back to reality, but it comes out in clumps, the strands separating from my scalp. I touch another patch and the roots break. With a blurry vision, I look up just to find my reflection smiling. But I didn't smile, how can I smile with my face tearing apart?

I stumble back.

The mirror calls me. As unnerving it is, it is scaringly enchanting - the way it seems to call me closer and closer.

The voices scream. A hand wraps around my throat, choking me. I thrash, claw at the air.

No.

It's just in my head.

Just in my head.

I somehow tear myself free and run. I lock myself inside the closet, gasping for air. The door rattles, a fist slamming against the wood.

No.

No, please.

I count my fingers. I count them again.

The banging grows louder, the voices shrieking.

I reach for the safe. My vision is too blurred to dial the code. The door shudders, cracking at the hinges.

No.

I try again.

The lock clicks.

I wrench it open and reach inside. My trembling fingers close around cold metal. A familiar paper drops to the ground, but I don't look at it. My hands hurt. The blisters burn, stinging along with every being of my existence. Is this what I was made for?

How can I protect a child when I can't protect myself?

I cock the gun, its weight anchoring my resolve.

I force myself to see her one last time, desperate to have one last look. But the harder I try, the more she disintegrates. Samara–

The door crashes open.

I pull the trigger.

23 February 2018

Mother,

Everyone hates me. And I can't even blame them—I hate myself too. I despise my existence, every inch of it. Why aren't you here? ~~Why do I even bother writing to you when I know you'll never answer?~~ You were meant to be my mother— the one person who would love me, care for, and be there for me no matter what

You were meant to be here.

But you left. You left me alone with a life I never asked for. I don't wish to be here.

I know you were suffering; I know the pain must have been unbearable. But that doesn't change the fact that you abandoned me. Nothing, absolutely nothing, gave you the right to leave me behind, to let me face this world full of pain alone.

~~I love you, but the worst part is~~ I don't know what loving you looks like. I've never felt the warmth, the comfort, or the safety of a mother's love. How can I be so hopelessly in love with someone who shattered me completely? Someone who broke me into pieces, then left without putting me back together.

Someone who couldn't stay to love me back?

Everyone says I look like you. Some say it with disdain, like I'm a cheaper version. Others say it with strange relief, as if I'm the last remnant of you, they're happy still exists.

 I'm in the shadow of what you looked like. In pictures, you were beautiful.

As a child, I wanted to look like you. I wanted to be graceful, like you looked in every snapshot.

And it happened. You reside within me somehow, etched into every part of my being.

Every resemblance is a reminder of how you failed me and how you tore me apart with your absence. I don't want to be like you. I don't want to be your shadow.

Maybe you're at peace now. Maybe it was better for you to leave; you didn't have to go through more of the reality this hell is glorified to be.

But I will not forgive you for leaving me here. I don't think I ever can.

I want you to feel the pain of being the one who lost all pain.

4 May 2020

Mother,

Every breath physically hurts. I'm not sure whether I know how to keep going. I want to stop. I want to end all of this— But I can't. Because that would make me like you, and I can't be like you. It's so hard. Fighting the things, I want to scream at and destroy.

I am unaware of what love is.

I am utterly unaware of what it feels like to be loved or to give a love that doesn't come wrapped in altering pain.

I miss you. I don't know how to stop missing you, how to stop wanting you, when every fibre of my being craves your unfamiliar warmth.

Sometimes my feelings overflow.

I feel nothing at all.

You left me so you could find peace. But if that's the only way you found yours, then I'm terrified I might never find mine.

November 11, 2023

Samara

I stand in front of this old mirror, its edges dulled by time, but I stand in front of it as if it is a grand vanity in some opulent ballroom, as if I were something worthy of admiration.

I smooth down the fabric of the dress hugging my body- black, with an undertone of aged wine, which, oddly enough, looks flattering on me. My eyes are edged with deep strokes of kohl – giving it a Taylor Momsen touch, as Kaya likes to call it. My father wouldn't approve. He probably thinks I'm into satanic rituals. Not that I mind.

He is out of town for the week, and, it feels like the universe suddenly has decided to cut me some slack, letting it line up perfectly with the annual Socials event.

One night, when I'm not intoxicated and can exist outside the expectations placed one me.

This evening is different compared to our other events.

This is the night when our campus turns into something like a coming-of-age film, as we join the neighbouring boy's college. It's not a prom but feels close enough to let us indulge in the fantasy.

As I move out by the back gate of my apartment building, I see Kaya waiting for me, next to a cab. I take a moment to appreciate her. She looks luminous under the glow of the artificial streetlight with her dark hair falling effortlessly down the back of her pastel pink silk dress, the colour complementing her pale skin, and I think to myself that an endearing beauty like her could easily charm her way into the world.

For about two years now we've been neighbours and batchmates.

Our friendship isn't perfect- far from it. We argue, fight, drift apart sometimes. But when it matters, she always shows up. She is the one who holds my hand when no one else even notices I need it. She is the only friend I have, I appreciate every second of her presence, I love her.

As I walk up to her, she grins, her eyes sparkling with playful amazement.

"The sun clearly hasn't set yet. I'm blinded by its light. Oh wait, never mind, it's just you," she says, circling me like a moth to a flame.

But the thing about flames is that they don't ask to be worshipped. They only know how to burn.

And the thing about moths?

They don't chase the fire to die. They chase it because it is the only light they have ever known.

I tuck a loose strand of hair behind my ear, closing my eyes for a moment to shake off the thought.

I pull out my compact mirror to adjust my mascara. And the reflection staring back at me doesn't even feel like mine. My eyeliner is sharper than my usual shaky hand can manage, and the blush covers my freckles.

I blink at the woman in the mirror— the resemblance guts me. I quickly break the gaze, fishing around in my sling for the lip gloss.

Kaya watches me carefully, head tilted.

"I wish I had even half your confidence. You just... glow. I want that." Her tone softens, a hint of vulnerability slipping through the usual bravado.

It's the moth's love for the flame that kills it.

The flame never asked to be loved.

Life doesn't work the way we think it does. Sometimes, we learn something, and just when we think we've mastered it, life shuffles its cards and we realize, there are more ways to play a game than the one we choose. It doesn't make us an experienced gambler, one with millions of dollars in their bank accounts, it just makes us a player.

And players don't win at life.

Gamblers do.

Maybe it wasn't the moth after all.

She will find out eventually.

I click the lip gloss shut. Turning to her with deliberate patience, I speak, my voice soft yet almost admonishing, like a mother's,

"All of us are different, Kaya, you think you're not as beautiful as anybody else, but in all honesty, you wouldn't have been able to admire the beauty in someone else , if it wasn't there within you. Stop being so hard on yourself. You're stunning. You could outshine anyone, any day."

I lean back a bit. "As for the confidence, I fake it, people can't really tell the difference"

With a sigh she smiles, "Yeah, that... I know."

She would think about this for a while as she laid down at night.

That is where all life changing decisions are made subconsciously, immediately before falling asleep.

I hope kaya can finally learn to love herself.

I wish I would learn to love myself too, one day.

Hope is a treacherous thing.

As she reaches for the door, her eyes snag on something. My wrist.

Before I can pull away, her fingers curl around my arm, it isn't a forceful grip, but it is not gentle either.

Panic surges through my body, until I feel it jolt the nerve endings of my fingertips, then, as if conducting electricity, it reaches the very ends of my toes.

Calm down, Samara.

"What's this?" Her voice is tight, as her fingers brush the bandage just below my palm. Her eyes wide, any other occasion, and I would have thought she's surprised. Right now, she is rather shocked.

With practiced ease, I pull my hand back, brushing it off. "Oh, that?" I laugh. "You know how clumsy I am with razors."

I see the exact moment the air between us shifts. Kaya doesn't say anything, but I can feel her eyes on me, searching for something I am not about to give. I turn back to the mirror, with blurred vision, busying myself again, even as my hand trembles ever so slightly.

"Is it what I think it- ", Kaya starts.

"I'm bored, let's get going already", I cut her off.

The moth was dead.

Kaya doesn't press. She never does. But the way she looks at me then, makes something tighten in my chest. If it is pity, my heart would shatter.

Or more like, the remains of what once was, my heart.

The flame flickered for the last time.

I force a genuine, apologetic smile and sling my purse over my shoulder. "Come on, wouldn't want to miss out on all the fun now, would we?"

The moth was always doomed. Not by the fire.

But by the need to reach it.

30 June 2024

Samara,

"Every profound spirit needs a mask"

For as long as I can remember, I was a quiet child. I wasn't afraid of speaking; I just never saw the need. Words felt like clutter, spilling out of people mindlessly. I read one of Erickson's books as a young boy and was beyond fascinated.

Thereafter, I preferred to watch. People reveal themselves when they think no one's looking.

I'd sit on the edge or stand in the corner of rooms, listening and watching. Silence is where the world eases off for you to view it.

That habit never left me.

When I first saw you, I didn't find you extraordinary in the way stories like to paint people.

You reminded me of the philosophers I had spent too many nights reading. They talk about the duality of human existence, how we're all two things at once: the person we present to the world and the truth we bury deep inside. For me, you were that duality incarnate.

A paradox one can never resolve, only marvel at. Open but guarded, vulnerable yet untouchable.

I did always find you beautiful, though. The kind of beautiful that holds your gaze.

Bewitching.

The quiet softness of your face and the delicacy of your skin parallel to the faint scars on your hands and your eyes betraying it all.

The more I watched you, the more I saw the things you tried to hide: the way your hands tensed when I got too close, the flicker of fear in your eyes, before you smiled and played along.

So much effort behind, so much ease, as if trying to fill the space that might otherwise swallow you.

It's hard to explain.

You felt like a mystery, cradling me in your weary hands, only to let me slip away

like the wind, free yet heavy with buried lies.

Like the sea, free yet bound by the hues of the sky.

You found your way into me, in gentle, sweet moments that built on one another, like a pyramid.

The philosophers would call it an obsession. The poets would call it love. I don't know what it is, but it feels like insanity.

I didn't fall for you; I studied you, memorized you, convinced myself it wasn't some notion of love, only to be absorbed by your being.

I was the sea, spellbound and consuming, absorbing the aurora of your sky.

You're a part of me—have been ever since we met and will be till my dying day.

To let you go would be to erase a part of myself, and perhaps that's why I can't.

Every day, I feel you keep getting farther away from me, yet I find myself getting closer to you.

Like the seashore, where the receding water leaves the sand crying out in thirst and parched. I love you more and more with every passing second, with every breath I take in—more than before, more than ever, more than I could consume.

I know, oh I know, you'd come back.

Rain, and I'll soak in.

This suffering feels like a hell I cannot escape, and the one awaiting me in death will be no different, I'm sure—for the only heaven I seek is you.

17 November 2020

Mother,

When you're driving, the road doesn't always stay smooth and clear. Sometimes you run into traffic that just won't budge. It feels like you're stuck, trapped in a moment that drags on forever. In those times, all the fragments of freedom pierce your heart with overwhelming intensity. You feel it in your chest, a tightness brought on by rising frustration. You might even hit ~~yourself,~~ your steering wheel or window in frustration. Might silently scream, grind your molars, or, more naturally, curse. But none of it helps. You're just stuck. Time creeps along, second by second.

You don't make peace with it, but you try to compose yourself. Still, all you feel is the weight of impotence and the suppressing ache of life momentarily out of your control. That's what dissociation feels like. It's not just emptiness; it's a sore, painful void. You detach from the world, cutting yourself off from everything, convincing your mind that it's better this way. You try to breathe and tell yourself it won't last. Sometimes, for a moment, you find a bit of calm, like convincing yourself that the traffic isn't so bad. But then, out of the blue, it hits you again—all at once. A wave of emotions and memories you thought you had escaped sweeps over you, consumes you whole, and there's nothing you can do about it but slowly feel it tear you apart.

You find yourself in the wake of a heartless paradox.

Two brutal, conflicting desires.

Certain parts of you want to feel nothing, escape the void, and avoid the heaviness, unable to bear it anymore. And yet another part wants to feel everything, devour it whole, and connect with life, to hold on to even the smallest, most fragile attachments. You're stuck between wanting to numb it all and the craving to fully experience everything around you, to perceive the entirety and find clarity. It's infuriating. It's like standing in a storm, arms wide open, wishing for the rain to stop but also yearning to let it soak you.

For you might find warmth in the icy stings of those raindrops.

This is part of being human, the struggle between wanting to escape while fearing pain and also needing to feel alive. Dissociation doesn't just cut you off from reality; it confronts you with the deepest of your truths. We're fragile beings, longing for peace, yet we're shaped by the chaos we withstand. Perhaps, in all these tough moments, when you keep going even though it's hard, you find tiny pieces of yourself.

It's not always about simplicity, but about perseverance.

November 11, 2023

Samara

Leaning against the counter, I feel my back protest after two whole hours of keeping up with the charade. Time drags on when you're forcing yourself to smile. I can't seem to remember why I wanted to come here in the first place.

Some days, I crave distance from home so intensely that I don't stop to consider the people I'd have to face beyond its walls.

Especially now when Kaya has conveniently disappeared onto the dance floor.

How predictable.

I shouldn't have come.

Now, I am stranded with a group of my batch mates wrapped up in a game of Never Have I Ever. Can anything be more excruciating? I loathe this part of social events—the awkward questions, fake laughs, and eager over sharing. Usually, I can fake it. Flash a smile, show off the dimples, play the role. But tonight, I feel sick. My back aches and even pretending feels Herculean.

I drop the act of trying to get along when I clearly don't want to and let myself relax, leaning against the counter and scrolling through photos of Cersei —my beloved cat. Well technically my aunt's, but I spend more time with her than my father.

"Don't you have an image to maintain?" a deep, unmistakably condescending voice cuts through my bubble.

I know that voice.

A week ago, he was forced to read his impromptu piece at the literary club. The topic was "deadly sins" and he spoke something about the dichotomy of sin.

"What you worship is what you sin to become.

You learn to hate from the one you love beyond reason..."

His words had pulled me in before I even realized I wasn't present in my mind. I had been transfixed, watching the way his fingers flexed around his phone, the casual detachment with which he spoke of things that felt deeply personal.

I was utterly absorbed in the topic, until Kaya nudged my shoulder, pulling me from whatever blasphemous spell I had fallen under. When I turned, he was already back in his usual seat, his piercing eyes on me.

The ambiguous intensity in his gaze was invasive. I felt my skin prickle and it wasn't exactly pleasant.

I held his stare for a second longer than necessary, then abruptly got up and walked away.

I walked away because somehow, I felt vulnerable under his stare.

No, I walked away just because the arrogance in his stance was insufferable. Infuriating. That's it.

After that, his gaze would follow me often. And each time, it felt as though he were speaking to some unseen part of me, without uttering a single word.

Kaya caught up with this and has been feeding me information about him in bits and pieces. I think they're mutuals.

He is a med student, like me. I have seen him before, mostly in passing, at sports events or skulking at the club. He doesn't like attention, it appears, but his reserved reputation attracts plenty of it.

And now, there he was, standing in front of me.

I look up at him. Yes, I look up, because he possesses a stature that commands attention and a rugged build, the kind that makes one feel small, even when they aren't.

His eyes are a rich shade of brown, inky hair reaching his nape, roughly slicked back as if reflecting his personality. One look at him and you can make out he is the kind of person who has absolute disregard for others.

My fingers twitch at my sides. Unfair.

And right now, he's invading my space, so close, a soft scent of caramel and cinnamon envelops me and seizes my lungs. I hate that I notice it.

Men apparently have this infuriating habit of ruining their charms the moment they open their mouth.

Him however, I haven't heard him ever speaking without absolute necessity.

Snapping my phone shut, I raise an amused eyebrow, "Wow, you talk? I thought you communicated exclusively in brooding stares."

"Only when I need to cut through someone's narcissism.", he shoots back.

"Says the guy lurking at a party like a budget vampire."

"At least I'm not glued to cat photos to avoid human interaction."

"I didn't know I was being watched. Forgive me, next time I'll put on a show for you. Also Excuse you, Cersei is a queen, deserving of my full attention."

"Forgiven, my Lannister queen."

"Oh, so you are cultured. I'm rather astonished."

"As cultured as a swine, love"

My brain stops. *Love?*

I tilt my head slightly to my right, "Did you just call me, 'love'?

"Guess I did"

"Are you planning on luring me in with that charming voice of yours and sell my kidney?", I blurt out without thinking. I am not necessarily liking this much.

"Trust me, if I had the choice, it won't be your kidney that I'd sell"

I snort. "You're delightful. Really. You should write greeting cards."

"Only if they're blank on the inside. Like you."

I'm unable to form a concrete response because the joke stabs me with conviction.

What adds to it is the smug smirk on his face as if he was anticipating this reaction all along.

As *if he wanted it.*

This is the first time we've spoken. There is no possible way he could see beyond the surface of me. He's just another man who mistakes provocation for depth.

And yet—

My chest tightens.

His audacity ran through me like a shovel digging up my long dead body.

"Have you always been this presumptuous?", I ask him, my tone, indifferent.

"Have you always been this predictable?", he flashes me an easy-going smile and its sort of pretty. What is wrong with me and why is he suddenly so intrigued by my presence?

Before I can answer, my phone buzzes. Father.

Panic rips me through me, tugging.

I glance at Rayan, advertising the best of my smiles,

"Before this conversation gets any more delightful, I'll tap out."

30 October 2021

Mother,

Being a daughter feels like being a handcrafted piece of broken art. Painted by others, carved to please, cut by their fury, and crushed by their expectations. It's like living on a ventilator—living on the mercy and charity of others. Dignity is a far-off dream, and freedom a mere illusion.

I'm not a woman; I'm a puppet, bound by their expectations. Entangled by these strings that seem to smother me slowly. ~~I could be everything, yet I'm reduced to nothing~~. I'm a mere object, a bare body, a frail being. I'm destined to be judged, desired, and, at the end of it all, discarded. In all sanctimonious faith and societal glory.

They say in this grand play of life, that role is mine. So, I try to fit into my costume. I starve me of myself.

How do I explain that I was not bound to this? I was not intended for containment.

I'm the child of nature, bound to explore.

I have disappointed my mother, the water.

The wind frowns as it passes by me.

The trees pity me; the soil absorbs my tears.

It hurts them to see their child so lost in this world.

I can live if they are merciful enough, even my death waits for their approval. Waiting for the ventilator to be switched off, for my oxygen mask to be removed.

I'm just a trophy to be discarded on a shelf that lays under dirt and dust, forgotten. But what they don't see is that I am a human, and all I want is some dignity.

Love.

I'm trying to grasp it hard, like a log of wood holding me from drowning in the ocean, but it seems to be drifting away.

Is being a woman just carrying the burden of your own existence and everyone's expectations? Is being a woman just being sentenced to live a 'happy life' with no happiness in it?

7 April 2022

Mother,

There's this weight that follows me all day. It's always there, just heavy and uncomfortable, like a constant pain. I'm used to it now, so I don't talk about it. It's just an annoyance, but one that feels real, like physical pain. Then at night, it morphs into something worse—a suffocating feeling that keeps me awake. My iron lungs breathe rust.

I love to sleep. ~~And I love whatever gets me there.~~ It's the only time my mind gets to stop, even just a little. When it's not spinning, turning, revolving on some invisible axis that never slows down, when the walls don't feel like they're closing in on me. It feels like I've been put on a timer—one that never ends. It just ticks and ticks and ticks, forcing me to keep going, to keep thinking, even when I'm so tired, literally exhausted, close to collapsing. When I can barely stand. My eyes refuse to stay open.

It feels like weights have been sewn onto my flesh, meant to drown me. As if a sack of cotton dipped into a bucket full of water. I'm so tired. I just want a place to lie down, to close my eyes, to breathe without feeling like I'm fighting. Feel the air around me and take it in instead of letting it suffocate me. I simply ache to lie down, to truly rest. Just once. Will that require me to plead? Please forgive me. Forgive me for stealing your years, for draining the life from you. Forgive me for existing when I never should have. Forgive me quietly, gently, within these silent whispers. Forgive me quietly, gently, within these silent whispers, and let me sleep.

November 11, 2023

Rayan

I don't believe in coincidences.

Everything's connected, purposely, beneath the surface.

To call something a surprise is just a way of running from reality.

Yet here I am, seeping in a certain coincidence, into my being.

The warm scent of cherry and coffee curls through the air, grounding me in the present, but my mind finds itself in the past.

There she is. Standing at the counter, mere inches away, lost in her phone.

Cat pictures? Seriously?

She's so deep in her phone; she hasn't sensed my presence yet.

Or she has and is deciding to remain oblivious.

Her hair, a rich shade of dark chocolate, falls in tousled waves, shorter strands framing her face.

I want to see what lines are creased on her pale face, but I'm behind, and shifting to the side feels too deliberate, too obvious. Yeah, I know how this looks—borderline stalkerish, but she doesn't have to know.

The memory from roughly two months back hits me hard.

I was driving home late, barely paying attention to traffic, blasting Muse.

But that night, something caught my gaze. A car driving alongside mine. Not the car. The girl in the backseat.

Her eyes.

That's the first thing I noticed.

Her head rested against the window, eyes staring into the void. She looked familiar, unsettlingly so. But I couldn't place her.

Tears streaked her flushed cheeks, escaping her dark lashes, glowing under the passing streetlights. The pain and conflict in her eyes was arduous. Her lips, pressed in a straight line, forcefully suppressing her sounds of grief. But silence, I've learned, is never passive.

It is a living thing.

It's stifling.

It is suffocating.

She looked like an angel burned by her own fire, *wings reduced to ash.*

Time seemed to pause for a minute as I watched the golden halo reflecting on her skin and the wild strands of her hair seemingly winged against the wind.

In the winds of autumn, she stood like a dying leaf, so elegant in her decay, as if surrendering to the fate written in its veins.

My grip tightened on the steering wheel, my chest getting heavy and I felt this overwhelming need to pull her away from it all.

To protect her from whatever seemed to be crushing her.

My hands ached for not being able to wrap them around her, hold her to me and know what's going on in her mind, to shush her thoughts. I wanted to find the source of that pain and tear it apart.

Watching her felt like gazing at the stars, in wonder. I could do it for hours, no matter how much eyes burned.

In that moment of isolated silence, I felt some twisted feeling of peace, the feeling that this is exactly where I want to be.

She shook her head slightly, muttered something to whoever was driving. Her expression soured. She didn't seem to like him much.

Hurriedly, she wiped her face with the back of her hand.

Her eyes–impossibly indulging–glanced toward my car.

They were the kind of eyes that looked through a person; they saw you, drew you in, pinned you in place without meaning to, and you could never look away.

No way she could see me through the tinted windows, but for a second, it felt like she did.

I felt bewitched.

In that moment, in all my 22 years of existence, I felt someone saw through me.

I had a desire to shield that someone away from the world and keep her to myself.

She rolled up her window and smiled. A brittle smile, the one you practice when you are alone. Some people say eyes are a reflection of one's soul, here she was smiling in front of me but her eyes were so empty, so hollow, looking at the fainted reflection of herself in the mirror and it was like she was putting on a façade but for once I could see the affliction behind it.

But even in her misery, she looked so beautiful, too sacred to possess, she could be mistaken for an impressionist piece of art.

All of a sudden, the car sped up, like a curtain falling, and just like that, she was gone. I tried to follow, but she disappeared between the traffic.

I was disheartened. I felt like a person disappointed after waking up from a pleasant dream.

That's when I realized. I'd seen her before. At the club.

We'd never talked, but she was hard to miss.

I haven't been able to forget her since.

I'm not the type to fixate, but something about her stuck. She crept in slowly, like erosion, the way water wears down stone.

So, seeing her here tonight, at our college socials? That's not random.

Not after weeks of observing her at the club.

I've noticed she's deliberate in everything— her words and her snobbishness, as if locking up her real self in the prison of her acts.

You can always find her smiling or sneering around, avoiding people like plague, carefully orchestrating every interaction. Every step she takes is a contradiction.

Although she doesn't like to overindulge, she's empathetic to a fault and cannot see anyone around her in any sort of agony.

She takes a cab to her residence every day, but also gets packets of food, which I discovered were for the homeless and the strays.

She seems genuinely happy whenever she does that and I can't help the rush of pride that I experience whenever I see her that way.

In the weeks I've been watching her, I've seen a girl who gives more than she takes.

I have seen a girl who wears her charm like armour, stitching a mask onto her face so seamlessly that no one ever thinks to look beneath it.

And I wonder—how much can a person break before they become *unbreakable?*

How much must be taken from someone to turn them into a *giver?*

And just how much pain must she carry to offer love so *generously?*

Two minutes ago, she was laughing with a group before abruptly cutting and closing off. Now? She's checked out.

She does that a lot. Space out, without realizing.

And before I can stop myself, I find myself standing right next to her, with the words leaving my mouth.

"Don't you have an image to maintain?"

She doesn't flinch, doesn't even look up. But the slight pause in her fingers as she scrolls through her phone tells me I've sparked up a fire that was smothered by a blanket.

And I just removed that blanket.

This feeling's mutual, you're making me nervous and jittery too Samara, if only you knew, this is unlike me, but so are coincidences, aren't they?

If only you knew, if only.

One day.

5 January, 2023

Mother,

Reduced to being a choice my entire life, I'm an orphan grasping at whatever I can find bereft of belonging, encased in a grave of my making.

I think I'm nothing but an afterthought, subjected to the decisions of others, never to the choices of my own.

I feel this desperate need to matter. To trick myself into believing I am more than I am. Just to satisfy the thirst to exist.

Being a disappointment is my hallmark of fame.

To live a life of charm disgracefully.

All this time, I thought I was afraid of losing people. But the truth is, I've only ever been afraid of losing myself to them. This constant need to be liked. To change myself piece by piece until I became barely recognizable—even to myself. It's excruciatingly exhausting.

To put on a mask they'd approve of, only to take it off and find I've shed my skin along with it.

How do I stop this mother?

November 11, 2023

Rayan

I follow her out toward the empty parking lot. Obviously, I'm not letting her leave like that alone.

No, I can't let her go.

Should I *let her go*?

I'll just make sure she gets a ride–from a distance. I'm about to turn toward the entrance when I hear her voice, tight with panic and restraint.

"Yes, Papa, I'm just about to sleep."

I listen closely. There's a pause before she continues in a lower tone.

"Yes, I'm sorry. I'll take care of that and sleep."

Another pause. Her voice trembles as if on the edge of tears.

"Yes, of course, it doesn't hurt. It's nothing. It was my fault."

More apologies roll out, before she finally hangs up.

Two minutes of silence pass, before I decide step closer. She flinches at my presence.

Her eyes shimmer with tears, one slipping down her flushed cheek.

"Are you okay?", I ask her.

"Allergic to dust," she mutters, rubbing her eyes. "Or maybe it's just you."

She turns away, and when she faces me again, her expression is perfectly composed.

That rehearsed smile reappears. But her glassy eyes draw me in ever so deeply.

Her eyes match her scent.

Her eyes are the exact same shade as her hair.

She is bewitching but her piercing eyes are the ones captivating you.

We stare at each other. This girl is a doll, I can bet she never blinks.

She fascinates me. It's creepy yet beautifully enticing. No, I didn't expect her to break down and cry. But I didn't expect her to bounce back with her usual sneers so easily, either.

"I just came to check on you. Make sure you got a ride, since-", I gesture at the empty surroundings, "you're alone."

"How sweet," she replies flatly. "Just FYI, I was with Kaya earlier and I'm booking a cab for now. You can go."

Who is Kaya? I don't remember seeing anyone with her. I might have missed it. "I can drop you," I offer.

"No."

She steps back and draws an imaginary line between us with her hand. "See this? A boundary. You've got that Ted Bundy vibe going. I'd like to live, thank you very much."

I snort. "What are you doing in med school? You should be in HR with those boundaries."

She relaxes a bit, leaning casually against a car hood. "Pleasing my father."

"What about your mother?" I ask.

I am being intrusive. If I was stalking her before, this was bordering on psychopathy now.

What am I doing?

The colour drains from her face. She closes her eyes for a brief second, collecting herself. Then, with forced nonchalance, she says, "She died."

I should drop it. But no, here I go again.

"How old were you?"

I half expected her to shut down, but to my surprise, she answers. "Seven months."

My mind races with possibilities, trying to piece together the strained relationship with her father. None of them are good.

I think about my own parents. Both lawyers, always swamped, but they made an effort. They tried to spend as much time with me as physically possible and gave me everything I ever wanted or needed. Some would call ours a good relationship even.

"Don't pity me," she snaps. "Plant a flower or something instead."

Do you think this is pity?

You have to be so oblivious to not see what it is.

"Pity is for the weak. Don't flatter yourself."

"Tomato, tomahto." She waves it off. "Anyway, what are you doing in medicine? Brooding personality finally found its niche?"

"I want to sell organs. High demand, low supply. Basic economics." I reply dryly, throwing her earlier sarcasm back.

She bursts out laughing, and for the first time, it's real. Her dimples peek out, and her smile reaches her eyes.

I tilt my head, observing, holding back my smile. In the moonlight, a soft halo outlines her sandy beige skin. Her eyes shimmer like sand under sunlight.

She looks ...stunning. And once again, I find myself trapped in the halo surrounding her.

It's a beauty of substance, intrigue, and subtlety. I feel like sand to her water, ever so slowly, eroding.

Muse.

A cold November wind brushes past us, and she shivers. Without thinking, I offer her the black coat draped over my arm. She eyes it, and then me.

I mirror her expression. Finally, she takes it and wraps it around her shoulders.

It swallows her frame and I can't help but notice how right and fitting it looks on her.

She tilts her head back to the night sky, her eyes gleaming with wonder.

I follow suit, seeking whatever it is that captivates her so, yet all I find is an empty sky—blackened smoke splashed with ashen. My eyes return to her, and in that instant, my obsession treks a painful peak, for in the abyss of this night, the only light I see is the one radiating from her gaze.

It is in this very moment that I feel my grip on reason slipping. The weight of my fixation crushes my spine. And despite the dread of something I cannot name-creeping up my spine, I cannot—will not—look away.

"Do you believe in God?" she asks suddenly, her voice, filled with curiosity.

I pause. I don't want to disappoint her, but I answer honestly. "I think belief in gods evolved to help humans cope with mortality. Gods mirror the cultures that create them. None have convinced me. So maybe I'm God, having a human experience."

She studies me for a moment, then shakes her head. "So philosophical. Bet you quote Nietzsche on first dates."

"Only if dessert's involved."

"You?"

"I used to."

"What changed?"

"I did."

But after she books a cab, she quickly shifts gears. "If you were an animal, what would you be?"

"You're awfully talkative," I remark. Not that I mind.

"Well, you followed me out here like a stalker. I'd rather know about my potential murderer, before I call the cops."

"And the cops would like to know what animal I'd rather be?", I ask her, but when her expression doesn't change, I think.

"Penguin."

She doubles over laughing. It's infectious, making me smile. Something tightens in my chest.

"Why a penguin?"

"They're loyal. Plus, I don't rock formal wear. What about you?"

She scoffs. "Fair. An Orca."

"Of course. Apex predator. Figures. What a hypocrite."

She gives me that glorious smile, with a hint of dimples.

I like that smile. *It's warm.*

This moment is special and I don't want to let it go. I'm the one that put that look there. She continues. "If you were a stripper, what would your song be?"

I narrow my eyes. She's dead serious.

"Hail to the King."

She looks oddly satisfied, as if granting approval. She's into metal, I believe.

"Death row meal?" she fires next.

"A cigarette."

I look at her expectantly.

She pauses, then says, "Hot chocolate. Though I'm sweet intolerant, it's the only thing I can handle."

I don't take this small confession for granted. I'm open to whatever she's willing to give me.

Her fingers fidget with my coat pocket, then stop. She pulls out a box of Davidoffs. She gives me a look, then surveys the lot. It's empty.

These are peak party hours.

She flips the box open, pulls one out, with her ring stacked fingers, and places it between her lips. Eyes locked on mine.

Without a word, I flick my lighter. She leans in, lights up, inhales deeply, and exhales slowly, into the cold air, staring into the distance. It reminds me of the time in the car.

Lost in thought, I barely notice when she offers me the cigarette.

We stand there, nothing but smoke between us.

Too soon, her cab arrives. She steps away, glancing back and nodding as her goodbye.

"I'll see you tomorrow outside the club," I called after her.

"I'm not going out with you." Her usual snobbishness returns.

"I didn't ask. Return my coat."

"Take it n–"

I cut her off, turn, and walked away.

Return my aching heart too.

1 July, 2024

Samara,

"There is always some madness in love. But there is also always some reason in madness."

I built walls to protect myself from the pain of losing you, but I realized too late that these walls are just an illusion of safety. I find myself trapped between the confines of my creation.

I miss you.

Conversely, even when you were right next to me, I missed you. I think, deep down, I always knew. You were there, but a part of you wasn't. Maybe it was the lack of faith in your eyes, the goodbye I always felt you were preparing for, fighting the impossible and inescapable struggle to find solace and understanding.

I'm to blame, too. You feel so far away from me. And I think I wasted the time we had. Where I should've been in the moment with you, I was already grieving the future without you. I missed you while I still had you. I missed you in the moments you were with me, for the moments you wouldn't be.

And now those moments feel like sand slipping through my fingers.

I miss you more. Every single day, I miss you so much more. I'd give anything to hear your voice again, to see you smile, in the way it lit up something happy, joyous inside me. I miss the way you existed, the way you filled space. I've started to question my reality. Are you real? Were you ever?

You once told me that love is nothing but an eternal delusion. But my love, sometimes, people choose to live in their crafted fiction.

If loving you was a lie, I told myself, then I'd choose to tell it again.

I bleed poison, belladonna.

I bleed till my love matches the red of my blush. He drags his strange consequences if his strange ways and I bleed love, belladonna. My sweet killer, he is lured by my beacon of pride, he stares into my life, belladonna, and he doesn't blithe me, but he does.

I bleed poison, belladonna. My sweet killer, he loves me, but I don't bleed into love for him, the lights, the faint feeling of sun, the dead of the night where I hand you the ashes of your favourite poet, me.

I bleed poison amour. I bleed poison belladonna.

~~I bleed poison my Cheri.~~

I bleed poison, mother.

November 12, 2023

Samara

I find the mirror staring back at me with what I can only describe as cruel mockery. I feel startled by the intensity of my emotions.

I wash my face, then proceed to dry it off with a pale pink towel that reminds me of the sickly colour of syrup.

I don't realise I have been standing in the bathroom for 10 minutes with the tap still on until Kaya calls out to me from the living room, asking if I'm okay. She insisted on staying at my place for the night. Telling her I'm fine, I rush out.

I try not to think about my reflection. I try not to think about my eyes and how much they haunt me. They're just wrong. Maybe they're too close together, or too far apart. The depth of my pupils comes across as quicksand to me, pulling me under with no pullback.

There is also the faint black around my lips to consider.

It's like rot.

As if all the vile words I wanted to say in the past, but never did, have accumulated around the edges of my mouth, turning black, the skin that once was ivory pale.

To me, I look like someone bedridden for weeks, someone who would burn if sunlight fell upon their skin.

What scares me about my reflection is not just me, it's also my mother. It's strange, I realise, how I used to pray to look like her. Now the thought of that makes me feel sick to my stomach.

Her pretty face.

Pretty, but only when she made it so.

Pretty, but ugly in every way that matters.

And now, here I am, in front of the same mirror, staring at the face I used to hate for being too plain and sometimes loved for being "pretty enough".

How would it feel to walk the world with no discernible identity? Am I bad for wishing away this part of myself I possess? Should I be grateful that apart from this face, apart from this shred of beauty, I seem to think that nothing else about me is valuable?

I enter the kitchen, make two cups of coffee haphazardly and slide the second cup across the table to Kaya. She seems oblivious to my internal meltdown, I observe. I'm grateful for it. The fact that I don't have to explain my misery to another person right now is something that sits well with me.

As I sit here, carefully sipping from the cup and flipping through a book, resting on the table in front of me, aptly titled 'Suicide' by Durkheim, I realise, not for the first time, that I have nothing, no anchor, no purpose. I also consider the fact that I'm unsure about living long enough for it to matter. My personal supply of oxygen has already transformed into carbon monoxide as far as my lungs are concerned. I only wonder if now is the right time to depart from this world.

Time truly is a bitch, making everything about itself.

Shouldn't it be my turn to make something grand about me for once? My death at my own hands, for instance.

After all, my life is the only thing I own completely.

Would others blame themselves in the aftermath? Would they walk around the world carrying guilt and regret brought on by my final decision for the rest of their lives?

Do I truly affect other people as much as they affect me? Probably not.

They'd move on, I decide. They will remain unaffected. And if that's how it ends, then is it truly worth the effort? Although I will not be a witness to my funeral, I still want quite a lot of people to be disturbed by my death. I don't think I can simply sacrifice 19 seasons of my existence to a lukewarm finale.

The coffee has gone cold before I'm done finishing it. I pour the remains into the sink, and

I get up to leave for the club after Kaya hugs me goodbye.

I think about her kindness and notice the untouched coffee mug on the table. She might have forgotten about it. I empty the remains into the sink, wondering if I was right about myself today.

And if what I'm about to do is right.

An hour later, my fingers trace the seams of Rayan's suit jacket, and a smile curves my lips. The memory of last night clings to me—Papa calling to ask if I was asleep and if my back still hurt when he shoved me into the floor, from when I breached the boundary and argued with him. I was so lost in that conversation; I didn't notice Rayan approaching until he was right there. He caught me off guard. I tried to fall back into the small talk, to play the part I always do, but I just didn't have the energy. Maybe I was too tired, or maybe I didn't want to pretend. So, I asked him things I was curious about.

And *he answered.*

Without *any sarcasm.*

Maybe he felt guilty after I mentioned my mom. I half-said it to make him shut up, but he didn't. He stayed, talking like it was nothing. The jacket was a sweet gesture, sure, but honestly, if he hadn't offered it, I wouldn't have bothered with him again. That's just basic manners, really. And no, I don't want him getting the wrong idea. I could've returned his jacket through Kaya, but after how humble he was last night, this feels like the least I could do. Especially after I didn't even thank him—and, well, I did steal one of his cigarettes. Not my fault, Davidoffs practically beg to be smoked.

Our literary club meets at Peddlers, a cafe that feels more like a storybook cottage—white fences, cozy corners, enough charm and aesthetics to feel like a home. We split the cost and book it three times a week for readings and events.

Stepping out of the cab, I spot Rayan across the street, casually leaning against his BMW. His tall frame is composed, broad shoulders draped in a dark sweatshirt, sleeves pushed up to reveal his veiny forearms and a dial watch. His dark hair falls in soft waves over his forehead, framing sharp cheekbones and a jawline too defined for someone who looks this calm.

His eyes, a brown so light, it can be mistaken for hazel, are always somewhat curious.

As soon as he sees me, he sees me, he starts walking, eating up the space in seconds and matching my pace without a word. We reach the gate, but instead of going in, he gestures towards the garden.

I narrow my eyes at him. But when he turns and walks ahead, I follow. We circle around to the back of the cafe, where a hooded staircase winds up to a sloped terrace. But Rayan stops, turning to me.

"Wait here."

Before I can ask why, he disappears around the corner. Waiting here is the last thing I should do, *yet I stay.*

The club activities are essentially boring anyways, and I just religiously attend to get some time away from home. I would rather avoid the forced interaction.

A minute later, Rayan returns with a large plastic bag. He pulls out a small shovel, and a rooted flower. What the...? It's a...daisy.

I blink. "Are you serious?"

He kneels at the edge of the garden, pressing the shovel into the dirt. "You told me to plant a flower. So, here I am. A man of my word."

I can't help the laugh that escapes me. And even after that, I can't suppress my smile. It's just sweet, is all, coming from this aloof person.

Shaking my head, I sit beside him, watching as he carefully digs a hole.

"A daisy? That's what you picked?"

He glances at me, a small smile grazing his lips, " Aren't they supposedly stardust or something? Hard to kill, delicate porcelain dolls."

I look at him for a beat too long while he continues to do his work.

Daisies are symbols of new beginnings, hope, and spiritual faith.

What an irony.

"Do you know the Greek legend associated with these?", I ask him.

He shakes his head, almost mechanically, and I continue, "During the Iron Age, humans got a little too obsessed with war, creating weapons left and right. After a while, Zeus got fed up and decided to wipe out the whole of mankind with a massive flood. Before that, though, the gods who had been living on Earth packed up and left. The last to go was Astraea. She was devastated by all the destruction, so she begged Zeus to turn her into a star.

When the flood finally receded, all that remained was mud and ruin. Astraea looked down at what was left and wept. Her tears, filled with sorrow, fell as stardust. And when they touched the earth, they– wait a second.

You brought up stardust earlier. You *knew* about this, didn't you?!"

He says nothing but shrugs.

I scoff, nudging his shoulder. "Charming."

We finish pressing the dirt around the flower and when we stand up and look down at it, I can practically feel myself radiating with pure happiness. "It looks..."

"Mesmerizing", Rayan completes.

I peek in his direction and find him staring at me.

My stomach flutters.

The wind blows, and several strands of my hair move across my face. Rayan focuses on them. His fingers whisper against my cheek, then down the sensitive skin on my neck as he brushes the strands over my shoulder. His touch tickles and burns at the same time.

Heat races to my face and my hands immediately cover my cheeks.

What the hell?

This unspeakable, overwhelming sense of...I don't know...I've not experienced it before...this feeling of...? Anyhow...it floods me.

Every part of me.

I brush the soil off his sweatshirt without thinking, then wipe the mud off my hands on it. He just chuckles, and I struggle to keep my expression blank.

He reaches back at the staircase, sitting on a step and then pats the empty space beside him.

I hesitate for exactly one second before placing my duffel on the higher step, spreading his coat over the cold stone, and sitting down beside him.

From here, the secluded garden stretches out beneath the open sky.

It's... peaceful in a way that feels so rare.

After a while, he pulls out a cigarette, holds it carefully by the filter, and places it between my lips.

Without a word, he lights it.

I inhale slowly. I know I shouldn't be here, but my body feels too heavy to move. So, I take another drag and hand the cigarette back to him.

We sit in grounding silence.

I watch the fading hues of the sky, the soft sway of the daisy in the breeze, and the mindless motion of our hands.

In my thoughts, time feels suspended, the world beyond this garden, out of focus. Until my reality slips in, and I eventually realize my two hours are up.

As I rise to my feet to leave, he tugs at my hand and gives me an envelope. I stare at him curiously, head tilted, to which he shrugs casually.

I don't know what's in it, and since I don't like being caught off-guard, I decide to open it later.

I lean in and tug it inside the pocket of his coat, the one I sat on earlier, and pick it up once again.

Our eyes meet for the briefest moment, and in that moment, I don't feel gratitude or some misguided flutter of affection, giving me butterflies.

What I feel is some twisted sort of comfort. For the first time in what feels like forever, I don't feel the need to explain myself or fill the silence.

I drape his coat around my shoulders and walk out.

Just like he did it yesterday.

He only smiles in return.

Human emotions are absurd. How easily can they go from despair and pure agony to ease?

On my way, I carefully peel off the rose-coloured seal from the dusky brown envelope. Inside is a small piece of folded paper with words written in black messy cursive.

They say if you stare into an abyss long enough, it stares back at you. I wonder if that's what the watcher craves. To be seen by the unknown. To be known by something deeper than themselves. I don't know if I'm writing this to you or for me. Either way, I think I've been staring too long. And I can't tell if I want to understand the ravine, uncover the mysteries or be consumed whole.

It's gut-wrenching, watching the ongoing annihilation of my defences.

13 November 2023

Mother,

How do I play the role of a lover if the bereavement of the child that was raised with my father's rage and my mother's silence isn't condemned yet?

How do I light the stage of a child that was loved before she became an antiquity of the teenage heart? the taste on my tongue matches the salted despair I shed; red is the colour of my blood without the fear that embellishes my untouched scars

My mother's endless glamour is the sword that moulds the marks all her favourite dresses are passed on to me, along with her voice in a glass jar burying all my dreams under the words that I yearn to utter but dare not, in fear of the glass shattering.

2 July 2024

Samara,

"Love is not consolation. It is light."

A mirror captures every detail with precision, as if sketching it in its memory. Water, however, creates an image that is restless, that a ripple can dissolve.

Both reflect the world but cannot possess it.

Do you think they envy each other?

He, the mirror, wonders what it's like to blur the boundaries between reality and a dream—a thirst for freedom.

While she, the water, longs to be seen plainly, wanting to feel the bliss of making something eternal.

It's possible they just stare at each other, awestruck, feeling the other is the better reflection of love.

The mirror's love is devoid of depth, while that of the water is all-abandoning.

A paradox of instability and permanence.

Tragic lovers bound by inception and fate.

A love of balance between holding on and letting go.

Everything carries its own beauty and its own pain.

So, *my Azur*, if you are the endless giver, I shall grasp and hold on to you endlessly.

Your pain, misery, absence, and presence- all of it is mine.

I'll let every inch of mine be tamed as yours.

I love you, and I'm never letting you go.

9 December 2023

Mother,

I can't function. I can't even close my eyes. My body aches the moment I lie down, like it's punishing me for trying to rest. My brain feels like it's tearing itself apart every time I try to think; my own thoughts turn into piercing needles. Tears sting the corners of my eyes. I feel scared because blood might drip down my eyes instead of salty tears.

It aches.

Everything hurts and I'm unaware of any way to stop it. I do not know if anything of 'me' resides within me anymore. It's as if I am filled with agony, I'm so tired of this pain. I'm so tired of living. This prison, which is so rightfully named as my life, despite being my own, seems inescapable.

I'm not going to share with anyone else the pain I foster.

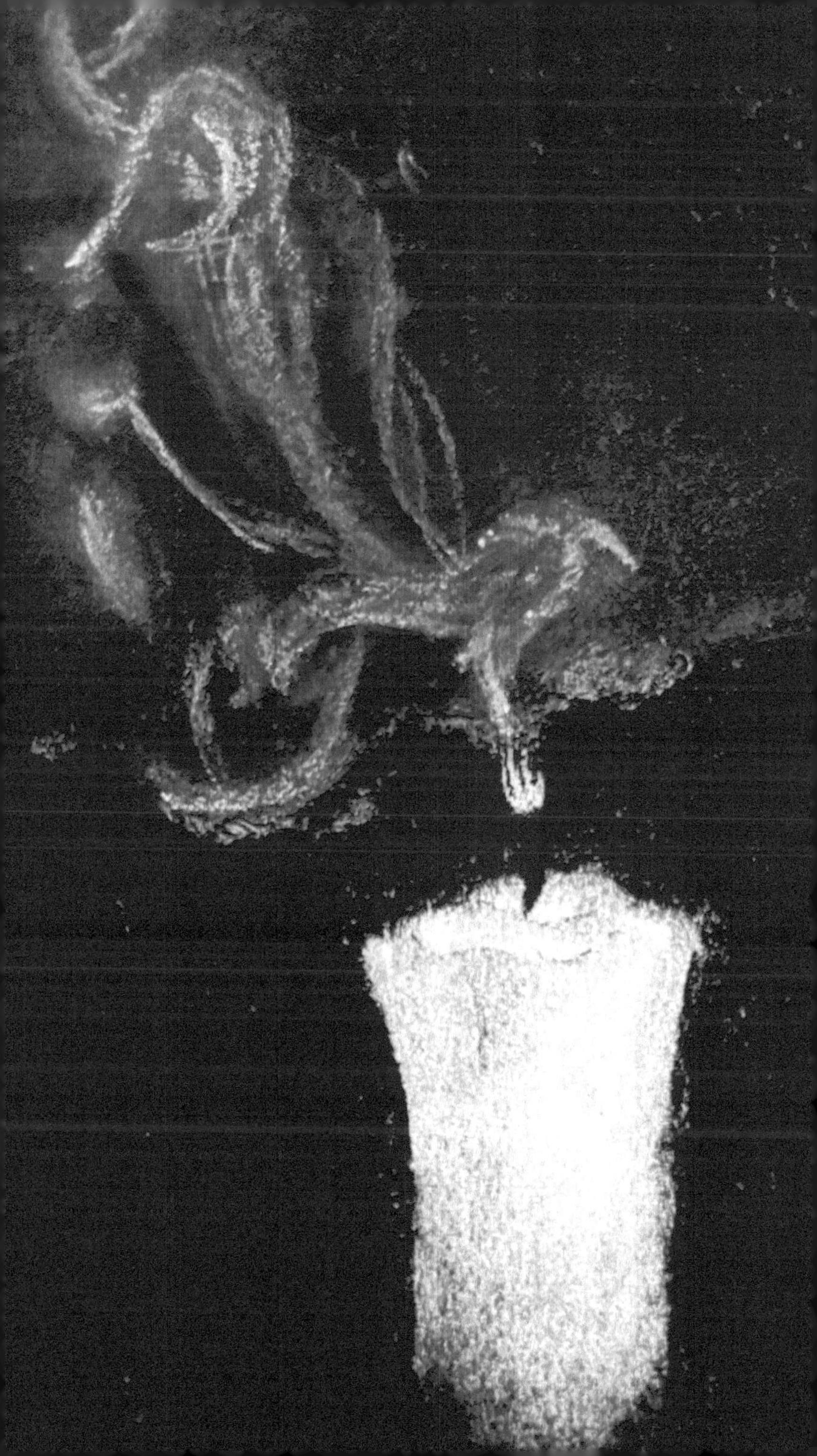

January 3, 2024

Samara

I open my eyes, surrendering to my lack of sleep, staring into the dark room.

Sleep feels like a melody I've forgotten the tune to. Especially when my body aches like this, fevered out.

Maybe it's the cold. Or maybe it's just me.

I don't bother with the jacket I should be wearing in a weather like this. A furry coat looks hideous over my carefully chosen clothes. Besides, warmth is irrelevant when the cold is rooted inside you.

Lately, though, it doesn't matter much. Rayan gives me his jacket whenever I forget mine, sometimes with a resigned shake of his head, other times so naturally, that I don't even notice until a smoky cinnamon scent envelopes me.

And now, I've started leaving mine behind more often.

Every day I return with one of his jackets, and each time I leave with another, as if I'm keeping something of him to hold on to later.

Earlier today, I felt too weak to go to the café, with the cold air threatening to bite me but I went anyway. Time with him feels numbered, and I would rather make the most of it.

I don't know what it is about him—this fixation he has towards me, or the one I'm starting to build for him.

It is terrifying, to be honest.

From the moment we met more than a month ago, there's been this thread connecting us. Still, I won't let my guard down. That would be foolish.

If he sees me for what I truly am, it will only hurt more. So, I'll let him exist on the surface of my life for now, like the sunlight slipping through winter clouds. It won't last forever.

Nothing ever does.

He immediately noticed how pale I looked today, his hand pressing to my forehead so suddenly I flinched. The warmth of his touch sent chills down my spine.

"You look terrible," he said, his voice laced with worry. "Let me take you home."

I gave him one of my fake smiles, shrugging off his concern. "Thank you very much, I can go myself."

He didn't argue, but the look in his eyes told me he wasn't convinced.

In a rehearsed gesture, he pulled off his Ferrari track jacket and draped it over me. I didn't need it, but when he narrowed his eyes, I gave in, once again, slipping my arms through the sleeves. It smelled like him. No way I'm giving that one back.

Oh, c'mon.

"Then I'll get you meds," he said in a firm tone.

I snorted, brushing him off, informing him I have all kinds of stuff at home.

"My father's a doctor. I'll ask him if it's serious." He doesn't care, I thought bitterly. He never does. I wouldn't bet my life on his concern. But what's one more lie in the pile I've built?

Rayan still didn't look convinced, though, and insisted I book a cab. I didn't have to, because my father recently asked the driver to chauffeur me everywhere and the car was right outside.

He watched me for a moment and before I could pull away, he took my phone, dialling his number and letting it ring.

"There," he muttered, handing it back with a smile. "Take care of yourself."

His smile always looks so warm and genuine, it melts something inside me. Why does it always feel like it's meant just for me?

Kaya stopped by to check on me some time later, and the moment she noticed the oversized jacket hanging off my shoulders, I could see the wheels turning in her head.

She crossed her arms, smirking. "That's not yours."

Ah, good lord. I exhaled, bracing myself. "No, it's not."

Her grin widened. "Whose?"

I hesitated. Kaya gasped, just for the sake of dramaturgy. "No way. Samara. Tell me this isn't Rayan's."

I rolled my eyes, but I could feel the heat creeping up my neck. "It's just a jacket, Kaya."

"Oh c'mon," she shot back, practically swooning. "This is, like, the present-day equivalent to courtship."

I shook my head telling her she's ridiculous, but she just sighed, "I'm glad, you know? That you have someone."

I swallowed; my skin suddenly too aware of the fabric between my fingers.

She continued, "it wouldn't be the worst thing in the world if you let yourself have this."

I didn't respond. Because she didn't understand—having something means having something to lose. It's like lighting a candle by the window, where the wind blows cold and free.

Now, hours later, I'm lying in bed, staring at the text from an unknown number.

How are you now?

Of course it's his. I haven't saved it yet, and I don't know if I will. I don't like texting, but I miss being there with him. Before I can stop myself, I hit the call button.

It rings once.

Twice.

I almost hang up, but then he answers.

"Samara?" His warm voice pulls me out of my hesitation.

"I'm better.", I say in a flat tone, answering his previous question.

"You don't sound better," he responds, as if he sees through every defence.

I don't reply, dodging his concern. "Why aren't you sleeping? It's past midnight."

"Mom, you didn't come and tuck me in."

I laugh despite myself, the sound so foreign it startles me.

"You should do that more often," he speaks. "You look beautiful."

My heart stumbles over itself at his words, and my hand moves absently to my face, as if trying to understand what he sees.

"Uhm?"

"You should laugh more," he repeats, his tone softer this time.

There's something in his voice that makes it feel less like a compliment and more like a plea.

I sigh, the weight of his words pressing into me. "There's not much to laugh about," I mutter, and then, almost reflexively, add, "Except you, of course."

"I can change that," he states, and the conviction in his voice once again makes me pause.

I don't answer. I don't know what to say.

No, he can't.

He can't change anything.

He cannot undo the losses that made me.

I was born into this fate, and it is hard, but I've made my peace with it. I've learned to live in the fleeting joyous moments, not expecting anything to last. Nerves vibrate in my stomach, and I take a deep breath and lie down back on the mattress.

As if sensing my silence, he pleads. "I'm here Samara. Are you really, okay?"

The question hangs in the air, marked with a sincerity I'm not used to.

I let myself believe he means it. That he always will. The thought terrifies me, but it also makes me feel less alone.

I swallow the lump in my throat. "Yes," I whisper.

I hear the rustle of sheets on his end, as if he's settling into bed.

"Can you stay?" The words escape me before I can second-guess them, trembling with all the fear I can't admit.

"As long as you'd want me to," he murmurs, and his voice is reassuring, like an anchor I can hold on to.

I close my eyes. Familiar wetness burning at the edges.

But this time it's not agony that brings them.

It's *dread.*

Dread that this moment, this closeness, is as fleeting as all the others. Someday, he'll see past the mirage and walk away.

He'll leave. They always do.

It's hard because there's a thousand things I want to say.

It's hard because I don't know what I feel, yet I want him to listen to me.

It's hard because I never thought I could be in love, let alone the thought of someone leaving even momentarily making me tear up.

I feel pathetic or maybe it's just I fear the person on the other end finding me pathetic.

But for now, he's here.

For now, I let myself believe his words. He's not here with me, but it feels like he's close. I don't feel alone.

I close my eyes, letting his voice drag me down into sleep, hoping against hope that, for once, something might stay.

1 February 2024

Mother,

The longer you live, the clearer it becomes that this world is built on pain, suffering, and futility. That's all that truly exists beneath the layers of delusion. Wherever there's light, there'll always be a shadow. For every victor, there's someone who's been defeated. The selfish intent to preserve peace? It starts wars. And hatred—hatred is born to protect love.

Love.

It's like a hidden fever, biting you through winter's heaviest armour—an illusion stitched together from fantasy. But when you really love something or someone, not just in theory, not just for the sake of saying it, but with a truth so raw it hurts, you realize you can never truly let it go. And with that clarity comes the ache: the ecstasy of the past, the emptiness of the present, and the guilt that settles in between.

What is death?

Is it the presence

of an absence,

of sanity—

slipping through your hands

like sand you borrowed from the

ocean

and never returned?

Or,

as a poet might say,

the wind carrying your unreturned

soils to the ocean—

a bit of it

carrying your soul.

Well,

I am no poet,

and to me, death

is the eater of hearts

and the salvation of divinity.

3 July 2024

Samara,

"Life is continually shedding something that wants to die."

Do you think death can pick apart bonds? Maybe yes, maybe no.

Some would say yes, others, including you, would lash out and claim it's impossible.

Foolish mortals devour your words with answers to questions you yourself asked.

But the truth is not in the answer.

It lies in the heart of the one who loves.

Would death silence the rhythm of your heart for the one you love?

Would it reduce you to ashes, vanishing into air, leaving nothing behind?

Or does her existence become your love for her?

Does her breath echo your love for her— even when you no longer breathe?

That is what love is.

What death can do—

is to pick apart bodies.

But not souls.

Not the souls that are tangled for eternity.

Because I recall: death is where eternity lies,

with arms wide open,

waiting for you to fall into it,

and close your eyes.

February 15, 2024

Rayan

She is an abstract concept.

I have long prided myself on reading people with ease. But she unsettles me.

There are moments when her eyes spill over with feeling, as though offering a direct path into the webs of her mind.

And then there are others—when they lock themselves away, hiding every last bit of emotion. Since the day we planted that flower, something has settled between us. I brushed off her sarcasm that first day, thinking nothing of it.

But that night, replaying the conversation in my head, I realized I couldn't let it slide. Maybe she liked flowers—just not the kind you pluck.

So, I planted one for her. And not once did I regret it because the way she smiled that day was worth everything.

There's a selfish satisfaction I feel every time I catch that radiant waning curve of her lips.

Her smile sends me into a state of *drizzlosis*.

The calmness and comfort one feels while listening to rainfall's ambience.

That's exactly what it is like.

Lately, it's been happening more often, though it falls as quickly as it comes.

Three months have passed, and we've fallen into a routine.

Every other day, we meet for two hours. On weekends, we plant flowers.

Daisies, naturally.

I can't help but associate them with her, not merely for her beauty, but for the way she endures, blooming even in the harshest of seasons.

Her style looks nonchalant —cropped sweatshirts with pants and boots, or a tank top swallowed by an oversized sweater.

Minimal makeup, but the kind that makes her eyes look subtly bigger. Her cheeks carry a natural flush, her lips touched by the nudist of colours. Her hair, always loose and that mascara, often smudged around the edges.

Every time it is like that, she's quieter than usual. I've been noticing it since the first day. That's why I started bringing her hot chocolate from the café near my place.

It somehow lifts her mood.

The first time though, she nearly refused, called me a wannabe, and said it was unnecessary. The next time, she made me drink half of it, even though I hate that sweet stuff. But she doesn't need to know that. Now, she just takes it with a small shake of her head. We also cut down smoking to once a week.

She's afraid of attachment and tends to push people away.

I see it in the way she pulls away, building walls.

Every time we're supposed to meet, I half expected her not to show up. But she always does. There's hesitation in her eyes, but she still comes.

Especially after she called me that first time.

She was hesitant at first, her voice uncertain, but when I promised her, I would stay, I heard the faintest sigh of relief on the other end.

She let her guard down and fell asleep on the call. And that was enough for me to not realize when I drifted off myself.

Since then, we call every night.

I wait for it—like clockwork, like some sacred sanity—but I never call her first.

I can't.

I don't want to intrude, to push her into something she's not ready for.

I need her to come to me, to choose to fight her demons, to let herself trust.

And a selfish part of me waits for that moment, every day.

I wait for her to call, to shatter the walls she's built, to let herself smile and know it's okay.

I want her to come to me, not because I've asked, but because she's decided *she can*.

It feels like we're trapped within an hourglass,

each grain of sand drifting down like desert dust,

lingering in the air, suspended between moments.

and time stretches endless –

endless as the wind over barren dunes.

I've started taking pictures of her. It began as a way to tease her when she got all snobbish and mighty, but maybe it had an ulterior motive.

Every time I pull out my phone, I go full burst mode. Recently, she dyed streaks of her hair crimson—it looks fluid and enchanting against the autumn browns.

I didn't comment, just smiled. But when she smiled back, all radiant, my heart nearly stopped.

Uh, oh

Realization hit me at that moment.

I had officially lost it.

We don't talk much. I don't like talking anyway. And the things I want to know, I don't want to push for.

I asked her the other day if she misses her mother.

She told me in a low blank voice, "I never knew her enough to miss her. If I want to see her, I just look in the mirror."

She tried to make it sound light. I couldn't help but see the vulnerability in her eyes.

Then she pulled out her phone and showed me a picture—an older version of herself. Same hair, same skin. But the woman's eyes were... empty.

Like Samara's, sometimes. I felt my migraine hit suddenly, my chest going heavy.

She tucked the photo away and whispered, "She was beautiful."

"You take after her," I mumbled, my fingers reaching to wipe a tear from her cheek. She didn't pull away. Yet when my skin gently brushed against hers, she flinched.

Slowly, she leaned in and rested her head gently on my shoulder. My breath stilled. If I could pause time, I would've frozen that moment and framed it.

Minutes passed, and then she tilted her head. "Do you think the sun is ever jealous of the moon?"

"Jealousy?" I scoff lightly before I tilt my head, fixing her with a stare. How does she even think of this stuff?

"No, I don't think the sun is jealous of the moon. Why would it?

They both know their place, don't they?"

She blinked, matching my stare. Her eyes look so much bigger. "Because the moon gets to watch the world sleep. It sees people at their most vulnerable."

I thought about that. "Maybe. But the sun brings everything, including those people, to life. Without it, wouldn't everything wither? Including the daisies."

"Sometimes I wonder which one I'd be". She whispered, as if speaking to herself.

The terrible tragedy inflicted on me is I don't know what goes on in that mind of hers.

"You're the moon."

Do you notice how I wait for you every single day?

Do you see how beautiful you are?

She looked straight at me with a gleam in her eyes. Then she rolled her eyes and mumbled, "You just fancy yourself to be the sun god."

I chuckled at that. "I don't need to fancy myself as anything, love. I am who I am. I like myself to be untouchable."

She hit me and laughed. "I swear to god, don't flatter yourself."

I might be the sun, but you're the one who makes the night worth anticipating.

I'm the idiot who keeps rising every day just to get a glimpse of you before you disappear.

I am the god, but you are the altar I worship at.

Two minutes later, she went back to her usual, "If you were a dinosaur, what would you be?"

Dead. That was my answer.

Yet I still think about answers that might make her laugh. I get the sense she doesn't do that often. When she laughs, I want to laugh. When she smiles, I want to smile. Hell, I want to be the one to make her smile.

She asked about my parents once, and I told her. In return, she mentioned her father was a cardiologist. Her voice tightened, and she shut down. I've learned to navigate around topics like that.

Today, she's late again. I'm scrolling through the few photos I have of her—somewhere in them, she's smiling. Not at me, but at the flowers. She treats them like people and has given them names.

There's —Cam, Sansa, Arya, Gloria, Ned, Jolene, Jam—

Her scent reaches me before she does. I look up, and there she is, rounding the corner.

She's wearing a burnt wine, off-shoulder sweater that flatters her skin tone, casual jeans, and boots. Even with covered hands, she wears bracelets and rings like they're sacred.

She settles in beside me naturally.

We talk about some random stuff here and there, and after some time I pull out a cigarette, holding it delicately by the filter, and place it between her lips.

"You know," I murmur, "they say sharing a cigarette is more intimate than a kiss."

She exhales slowly, glancing at me sideways. "That's poetic. Maybe people just didn't want to waste a cigarette. Or maybe they figured kisses are overrated."

For a minute, we're caught there, hanging in the moment, the space between us thinning. I inhale, and her sweet scent envelops me. As if on cue, we turn away.

She turns to me, her eyes shimmering. "You're smooth, you know that, huh? Spouting cliches all the time. It's annoying."

I smirk, leaning back on the stair, my fingers brushing against hers just slightly as I take the cigarette back. " Maybe, I just say what I mean, and you're not used to hearing the truth."

She watches the ember burn, the faint glow illuminating the sharp angles of her face, in the fading skylight. "People avoid truth for a reason. It burns."

I exhale slowly. " But you can't really feel alive without the burn, can you?"

She looks at me then, really looks, her eyes piercing. "And what if it's too much? What if the fire swallows you whole?"

Fire is captivating.

I reach out, gently brushing her hair away from her face, my leather jacket hanging loose on her shoulders, her breath hitches. "Then at least I'd know I burned for something real."

She shakes her head once again, laughing softly to herself "You're impossible."

She pulls the jacket tighter around herself, and I can't help but think how right it looks on her, just so perfect.

"Thank you," she whispers.

"For what?"

"For being here."

I meet her gaze. "I wouldn't know how not to."

I ask her what her favourite colour was. She tilts her head, her lips curling into a beautiful smile, and answers, "Red."

"Why red?" I question, half-expecting some poetic answer, possibly something about roses or sunsets.

She pauses, tracing her fingers over a streak of red in her hair–bright against the brown.

"Because it's everything," she trails off... "It's love and rage, life and death, the fire that warms and the one that destroys. It's blood that keeps you alive and blood that spills when you're not. Red is desire, fear, passion, hate–all at once. It's beautiful, don't you think?"

She doesn't wait for my response, just stares at the sky above, her eyes catching twilight–

red fading into the sky. I can't really tell if she sees something there or if she's just avoiding looking at me.

After a while she asks me the same question, to which I have the same answer.

"Why?"

Because red reminds me of you.

And, because red is for love.

Love, too, reminds me of you.

If only you could see the red of your being in mine.

You'd see how much I see through you and of you.

But I can't say any of that, so I divert the topic.

Later, after she left, I noticed something where she had been sitting—a red Davidoff box. I picked it up carefully. It felt heavier than it naturally should.

I opened it slowly, tilting it until something slid into my hand —a sterling silver bracelet, its oxidized surface catching the dim light. The design was simple, a thin rope-like band.

As I turned it over, my fingertips brushed against a cool, tiny metal plate on the underside.

I squinted, straining to decipher the delicate cursive engraved there.

Apricity

I stared at it for a long moment, then slipped it onto my wrist.

Inside the box, on the top flap, in the same delicate script, were the words:

Love, Samara.

She hit me like autumn. There's nothing I could have done but fall.

15 February 2024

Rayan,

I asked you today, if you feel the moon and the sun , they envy each other.

And you looked at me as if I was disturbed. ~~Yes, well that I absolutely am , but~~ do you know why I asked that?

I went to the beach once. It was nighttime, and as I sat on the shore, the fine grains of sand beneath me and the gentlest breeze surrounding me, right under the light of the moon, staring at the mild waves of the water,

I was captivated by the beauty of the moon and ocean's eternal love.

He, the ocean, embracing her untold mysteries while she, the moon, surrenders to his endless depths, knowing they'd never unify—no matter how much the moon appeals and veils, silently luring the sea towards her.

And no matter how violent the tides get and how high they rise. The ocean, like a canvas, waits for the moon to breathe silver into his existence.

To know that his muse, who sparks inspiration and is the catalyst for artistic brilliance, is loved by so many others must be so heart-breaking.

The mellifluous sound of the harsh waves—the cries of unmet expectations and unspoken desires.

They stare at each other with untamed passion, accepting the reality that the flames of their seraphic love were never meant to ignite. How they are destined to be together, but fate keeps them apart.

So obviously the sun is jealous of the moon.

Because he wishes to be loved, without having to burn.

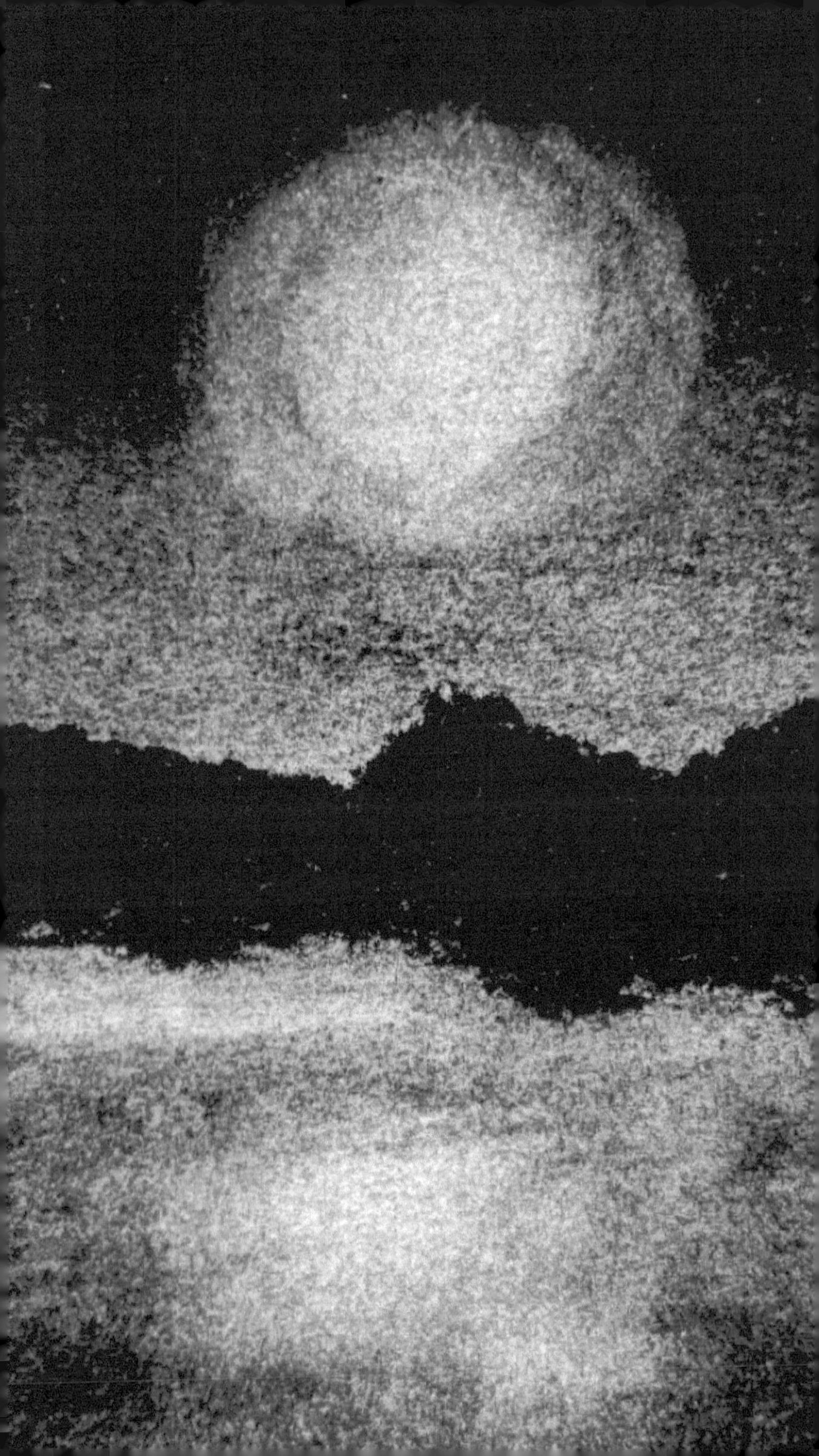

13 March 2024

Mother,

I was never forgiven. So why do they ask ME to forgive? How do they expect me to give what I've never received? Why must it always be me who rises above, who strives to be better, to become the saint? It hurts—no, it burns. It burns until nothing remains but ashes.

The tears I shed scorch my skin, and no matter how many times I blink,

The haze never clears.

The shards of pain return, sharper each time.

I can't do this anymore.

I want to run.

Run far away from this place, from these people, these shallow actors, pretending at joy.

Their laughter—Mother, it's unbearable. It's a scream drilling through my skull. I wish I could make it stop.

I wish I could tear it from the air, silence it forever. I hate them for their ease, for existing without the weight I carry. I hate it all. Everything. This hate—it grows, claws deeper, and it terrifies me. I don't recognize myself anymore.

There's something vile inside me, something vicious, coiled and waiting, whispering unspeakable things. I'm afraid of what I might do. Afraid of the temptation, how badly I want to follow it. I feel like setting the world on fire, watching it burn just to snuff out the sound of every shred of happiness that doesn't belong to me.

~~Maybe I was born wrong.~~

I am born wrong.

Insidious inside.

I think I'm losing my mind, Mother. I think everything is wrong. It's all so incredibly wrong. There's a sickness in me, something crawling under my skin, taking root in my heart. I swear, I didn't ask for this. I didn't ask to be torn down and rebuilt, only to be torn down again, but worse. Every time I try to crawl out of this pit, it feels as though someone breaks me at my very core, crumbling and crushing my insides.

And when I finally manage to stand, they blame me for wanting to run.

Should I search for who I am, or is that another lie sold to keep us reaching for something we'll never find?

What about morality, Mother? What is that, but a lie? An illusion dressed up as a universal truth. Forgiveness isn't healing me; it's scraping me raw, leaving me empty, filled only with grief. Crafted apologies, blades of remorse, and an inconsolable helplessness.

I look up at the sky, Mother, and it laughs and cries, as my chest falls and rises. This blackness keeps spreading, taking root in me like a rotting plant.

<h1 style="text-align:center">4 July 2024</h1>

Samara,

"Truth tends to reveal its highest wisdom in the guise of simplicity."

I am here, *my azur.*

Let it out.

Take it out on me.

Let that fire burn me,

For I'd be turned to ashes, yet those ashes would whisper your name– All of you.

Let me love.

May your wrath consume me whole.

Let me hold your hand– May they paint mine red with your blood,

The blood you claim is rotten and cold

Let me look in your eyes— May they tarnish me.

I won't ever forbid you.

Even with a knife stabbed into me by your hands,

I'll smile,

for I'll be close enough to study your face,

To feel your presence,

Your hands on my body,

To remind myself of your familiar warmth.

Love— To be next to you, even as we lie dead

With our plagued hearts.

APRIL 8, 2024

Samara

I wipe the smudged edges of mascara from beneath my eyes, catching my reflection in the mirror. The tears from earlier must've done it.

The car jerks slightly as the driver stops, pulling me back to the present. I quickly glance at myself—black A-line skater dress ending just above my knees, stockings, and my usual boots.

It's Kaya's birthday today, so I remind myself to pick up the cake later. Before opening the door, I slip off my rings and tuck them into my sling bag.

Months have passed and meeting him has become a ritual. I look forward to every other day with him, though in the beginning, I doubted it would last.

I kept waiting for him to cross a line or disappear, but gradually, whatever this is nestled within me, like a natural cadence.

He always brings me hot chocolate. I scolded him the first time, told him it wasn't necessary. Yet, he persists. God, it tastes awful–an insult to hot chocolate–but he tries.

So, I drink it, masking my grimace with a soft smile.

Lately, he's more talkative, sharing random bits of his day.

How he tried cooking and nearly burnt his kitchen down, how he hacked a friend's phone–though I was embarrassingly curious if that friend was a girl. It *wasn't*.

I don't have much to share in return, but his stories amuse me, so I cook up some just to tell him, or we just end up talking about gore tv shows and Japanese literature.

It's odd, realizing I study medicine to avoid disappointing my father, while he's genuinely fascinated by it.

I can see it in how he talks about surgeries, and the critical evaluations he assists.

I'm in my first year while he's in his last, doing his internship. There's something about the way he explains concepts when I'm stuck–pulling me in like a spell.

Maybe it's just his voice, but I could listen to him talk for hours.

He stopped bringing daisies after I practically begged him to.

The garden was full; anymore, and someone might step on them.

Now, he brings me a star jasmine every day from his garden.

Lately, I've felt this persistent urge to hold his hand.

This strange desire to feel his hand in mine, to thread my fingers through his, to hold on and not let go. I wonder why he hasn't. Maybe the time I flinched when he wiped my tears scared him.

But he's not the type to scare. Never mind him, I'll do it today, *if I feel like it.*

I spot him in his usual place, holding that familiar lidded cup and his lab coat. His eyes lift, scanning me head to toe, looking as if memorizing me.

He then gives me a smile and it looks so pretty, heat creeps along the back of my neck and marks my face.

I sit beside him as he hands me the flower and hot chocolate.

I take both, smiling.

One sip, ah yes, still terrible—and we slip into conversation.

Eventually, my head finds its place on his shoulder, and I smile when the heat of his skin radiates past his T-shirt onto my cheek.

Just like every other time, he falls quiet.

His hands rest carefully on his lap. And here it is again—that aching need to hold them.

I stare ahead, eyes locked on the fading sky, as if my composure depends on it. The air feels delicate, like it might break, and the seconds stretch unbearably long.

My heart beats loud in my chest, drowning out the world. His watch ticks, each second echoing in the silence between us. He sits there, calm, while this storm brews inside me.

My hand feels impossibly heavy. I start to move it but freeze, heat rushing to my face. What if he pulls away?

What if—God, what if he's gay?

But this can be platonic. Just holding hands can be a comfort gesture. *Right?*

I squeeze my eyes shut. The world won't end if he doesn't feel this too.

Pull yourself together, Samara.

And if he doesn't feel it—if he doesn't feel this aching absence and longing—I hope he drowns in it.

I hope he dies in misery.

The thought makes me chuckle. And that's when he looks down at me. He's so close, I feel his breath, warm on my skin.

Without thinking, my hand lifts, hovering halfway between us—palm up, suspended. He glances at it.

Without any hesitation he bridges the distance, like he's been waiting.

Our fingers brush, sending a soft shiver through me. Then they intertwine, slow and certain, like they were always meant to.

It feels... so right.

Not obsession, not infatuation—just raw, pure intimacy.

A connection that runs deeper than words, through blood. My hand fits too easily into his. I tighten my grip slightly; afraid the moment will be over far too soon.

This isn't love, I tell myself, but it's something just as fierce.

A need to protect him, to keep him here, safe, wrapped in the better parts of me.

Between walls painted with devotion, freedom, and something that feels dangerously close to possession. The ecstasy of this simple moment feels terrifying, like it could consume me. I feel breakable, yet completely safe.

He's precious and I want to shield him from myself but at the same time hold him close to me.

I close my eyes, tears pricking. I wish I could stay here forever. I think I whisper it aloud because before I can even process, he leans down and presses a soft kiss to the top of my head.

His thumb moves across the top of my hands and every single cell of my being becomes electrical.

The walls I built to protect myself crumble and comfort sets in as the iciness I've clung to for so long melts.

Metallica is right, for now, *nothing else matters.*

9 April 2024

Mother,

How relentless is love? Is it merely to lay bare in the open, allowing someone to endlessly devour your flesh? Feeding on your essence as if to own you, to possess you whole? I have little understanding of what it truly is, but somehow, it feels as though you've bestowed it upon me. (A sinker's last resort.) A blessing, just as his name implies.

Another of my compulsions, this time, I can't let it go. I can't let him go. He has invaded my space in such a way that he feels sewn into my being, and I can't seem to pull a single thread without risking unravelling everything.

He's the first person who's listened to me without trying to fix me. He looks at me as if I'm an empty canvas, and so ardently, as if he desires to paint every subtle detail of my existence in my presence. He holds my hand as though I'm fluid, the smoke from his cigarette slipping through his fingers. And me? I'm just perpetually searching for an opening, a way to escape, but he won't let me.

The smoke of his cigarette vanishing into the air—couldn't that be me, Mother?

His eyes, Mother, they seem tranquil, entrancing browns under the sun; sometimes, I feel they're the prettiest I've ever seen—~~seldom humorous, carrying so much curiosity and hope.~~

 It's somewhat suffocating; from time to time, I just want to gouge them out for not seeing the lack of feeling in mine. Rayan wants to give me a love of slaughter, but all I've ever felt is hunger, hatred, and pain.

I know that someone capable of fierce animosity is equally capable of absolute devotion. I just feel this burning need to protect him from the vile in me and from the people like me. How can I ever tell him that the only thing alive in me is the absence of a dead person?

My torment would swallow him whole, or maybe his love would consume me.

And, oh, how I wish to be consumed, to be devoured whole, to be understood. But I fear bringing him to his demise in the process.

I don't want him to fill the voids within me and call that love, only to shamelessly turn away once it absorbs him completely.

Loving something mortal is inherently meaningless—another feral compassion, like the moon, atrociously pulling the water toward it, knowing it's unattainable. But that is the mortality of existence, isn't it?

I don't want to leave him. Most of all, I'm not sure I know how to leave. Mother, I don't know how to stay, or if I should stay.

I don't know if it's better for him if I stay.

~~I do not know if I love him, nor do I wish to come to any conclusions.~~

All I know is, I want to sit with him, as we often do—his hand wrapped around mine, my head resting on his shoulder, sharing a cigarette, the ashes bringing solace to my heart. A time I wish I could freeze—something that could stand still.

A time that overshadows even the appeal of death.

5 July 2024

Samara,

"There are no beautiful surfaces without a terrible depth."

You are woven into my soul,

And I don't think I can ever untangle you.

You are all I am— A missing rib, a silent cry, a fallen whisper.

I love you dangerously,

So much that it hurts me every time I can't recall how your laugh sounds.

Not the one you forced,

But the one you let out genuinely,

Because, for once, you felt safe with me.

I ache to exist through you.

All these letters– Words left unsaid–

These walls of my room that I am confined in know your name.

They call for you. They search for you in every piece of me,

In every remnant I have collected of you.

Awaitance is a demon that devours your heart like a forsaken piece of religion,

piece by piece,

Gradually, relentlessly.

Every night, I think of you–

Of that smile of yours that reaches up to your eyes,

Your dark eyes, Brown and burning with a fire that lives inside,

Screaming to come out.

2 May 2024

Mother,

Suffering feels endless.

Nothing makes sense to me anymore, not one thing. Every day, there's this moment where it all feels too much, like I can't keep going. I just want to cry, to break down completely. ~~I want someone to hold me, to hear me, to understand me. I just want to feel known, cared for, and safe. And I have someone. But I can't go to him.~~

No matter what, we all scatter in the end. Everything we do, every bit of effort—it all feels pointless.

I'm stuck here, torn between pushing forward and giving up entirely. So, I close my eyes and, for once, try to imagine a world that's happier, one that feels lighter.

I dream.

The vanity of hysteria.

June 17, 2024

Samara

We're singing *Yesterday* by *The Beatles*—or more like I am, and he's just watching me.

His eyes don't leave me, like he's reading every word I mouth, but then I glance at the time. It's later than usual. It's always later these days. I give him a small knowing smile and stand up.

He doesn't let go. His grip tightens like he's holding onto something slipping away. Yeah, Rayan, I know. I don't want to leave either.

But I *must*.

And every passing day, it gets harder.

He looks devastatingly beautiful when he tilts his head slightly, navy blue shirt, staring at me like I'm the only tether he has to a foreign world.

I tug gently at his hand, pleading with my eyes.

Slowly, he rises, but his grip doesn't falter. He walks me out, fingers still laced with mine. We turn the corner, and he leans down, brushing a soft kiss on my forehead, the contact sending shivers sinking into my skin.

But I freeze.

The air turns to glass in my lungs.

My father stands right outside the café, his eyes on me.

His face is calm, disturbingly so, his eyes pitch black. But I know better. I know his patient rage.

I drop Rayan's hand like it scorches me.

I don't look back.

I walk toward my father because his wrath is mine to bear—not Rayan's.

My suffering and rapture are two separate, distant worlds.

Each step toward him feels heavier. It feels like I'm sinking into molten steel. My heart pounds against my rib cage, making it difficult to breathe. By the time I reach the car, I am drowning in invisible waves. My father slides into the front seat in silence. The quiet is asphyxiating. I don't dare turn back. I can't let Rayan see me crumbling. I slip into the car, and I choke.

Later, I stand in the drawing room beside my father. My lips tremble. I know what's coming.

My father hates when I do something other than what I'm supposed to.

My father believes I'll end up losing my mind as well.

He believes he is protecting me.

Believes.

People say pain dulls over time—that you get used to it. Like walking on fire until your feet burn numb.

But it's never numb.

It's sharper every time, cutting you in places you didn't know could bleed so much.

Each blow carves something out of you, and the need to end it all grows feral. There's no one to save you.

Like there's no one to save me.

Not the mother who left me to rot. Not *anyone*.

I stare at him, through blurred eyes, searching for a trace of warmth that was never there. I search his face for anything human.

His grip clamps around my jaw, snapping me back. His voice slices through every coating of comfort I've built.

".....we're moving abroad by the end of the year. Since you clearly can't handle the one thing expected of you. How could you? You're too busy whoring around."

My father is ashamed of me—

Ashamed of what I was, what I am, and what I ever will be.

The mere thought appals my insides. I'm aghast at the idea of being stripped of my individuality once again. Most of all, I'm horrified at the prospect of leaving behind the one person who, in years, has truly understood me. I cannot leave Rayan behind. The words land harder than the slap that follows. My head whips sideways, the sting blooming across my skin. The heat of tears presses against my closed eyes.

Blind rage

Shame.

It coils in my veins.

I try to speak–just a breath of defence, not defiance – but his fist answers first.

I glance at him, but my eyes drop just as fast. If I hold his gaze for even a second longer, everything I've buried–my anger, my exhaustion, my truth–will explode.

And that truth would scorch every belief he holds about me.

"You dare talk back?" he snarls. Then the belt comes down.

I want to run. From him. From my father. From the ghost of my mother. From myself.

His pitch-black eyes pin me down, and I tremble.

This will be the last time.

He steps closer. I focus on nothing, pretending to pick lint from my skirt. He's too close now. His breath, foul and hot, scrapes over my skin. I wish it would stop. Forever. His hand clamps onto my face, wrenching it upward. I can't. He forces it up until I think it would break, so I give in.

"How are you, baby girl?"

My cousin's voice slithers into my ears. It's been years, but it never changes. It's been years, yet it hurts differently each time. It's a sickness that built itself into my bones, cell by cell. Father loves him. He visits when Father's at the hospital to play with me, because I don't have any friends. He's eight years older. He has other people. I don't want to play this game anymore. I don't want anyone.

Please, Mom.

 Save me.

His sneer deepens. His fingers brush the bandage on my forehead.

"What's this? Papa hit you good, I see?"

Father didn't mean it. He was angry because I missed Mom. He works too hard, but he loves me.

He must.

My cousin laughs, shoving my head back. His mouth lands onto my neck, then my lips. His tongue forces its way in. I don't let him. I never do. He hits me then and I still don't. He fists my hair in one head and pulls them on the roots and I scream. Someday I'll be strong enough to push him off. Someday I won't cry.

His cold hands crawl over me. I disappear into my head. My twelfth birthday is five days away. I think of presents. I love gifts. Homework due tomorrow. Anything but this. Someday, maybe I'll tell my father. But he'd blame me. Like he blames me for Mother. He says she died because of me. But what if he's right. Maybe this is punishment. Maybe this is what I deserve. And then his face shifts. My cousin's face blurs into my father's.

A belt cuts through the air, searing my skin. It burns

Another.

Another.

I'm crying. My tears soak the floor, and I feel myself drowning in them. I am struggling for breath. Suddenly, a hand is helping me out of the water. Rayan's. Relief spreads through me like poison but as I come up for breath, familiar hands wrap around my neck, pushing me back. Mine. I look up to see my mother and choke on the words:

"Please, st—"

I wake up with a gasp. My palm bleeds from where I clawed it. Just a dream. Just a nightmare.

My face is wet. My wet shirt clings to me. I can't breathe.

My stomach cramps—it builds continually, twisting my insides to the point of implosion. I stumble from bed, my heart racing. I drag myself to the bathroom and stand under the cold shower.

As the water drenches my face, I catch a faint view of myself in the foggy mirror. The gentle downpour blurs my vision, its touch soft but chilling on my skin. It feels sacred, easing the rawness of my pain, the weight of my misery accumulated throughout all these years.

When that thought enters my mind, I close my eyes. I feel myself breaking apart, piece by piece, even as I stand intact, drenched and somehow still alive.

Blasphemous is the pretence of a mirror elicits, defying the downfall of water, making me sink into the abyss of conviction and existence.

19 June 2024

Mother,

Now and then, I end up consuming two packets of cigarettes in a blink of an eye. I don't want to; it's just that I have nothing worthwhile to do with these hands. I feel a sort of unease when they're idle, an anxiety so bad, like they're desperate to do something vile, to sin, but when I occupy them with something rather harmless, it's considered immoral as well. Father caught me the other day, and the disgust on his face was almost amusing. He called me depraved; well, that part I agree with, and declared it unethical—not for him, of course, but for me.

As if my weak lungs would somehow tarnish his whole bloodline.

As if my dark black lungs would make him infamous.

He is afraid of this heart? The very heart he won't be able to see even if I tear it out of my body and hold it in front of him to see.

He thinks my smoking is the reason behind my grades dropping, and honestly, it's hilarious. As if the bud is the one inking my papers.

Reasonably, I'm not in the state to take my book out and read a page without tears sweeping in my eyes, blurring the vision and spacing out. What's also funny is how he could see the ash on my lips but is blind to the one I've been crumbling into. He never noticed the bruises, the scars, the places I've hidden myself. Never saw the way I shivered at night, how my hands wouldn't stop trembling, how I'd look at him, my eyes red, begging , Find me, look at me, just love me. I'll be good. I'll be better. I'll be anything you want. Just hold me, I long for your understanding.

I think if I had looked at myself like that, I'd have ended up pitying myself.

But no, the only thing he's ever noticed is my failure.

My failing grades.

Not his trophy daughter anymore. Then he also saw me with Rayan in his eyes, that made me a whore. That, to me, again, was hilarious.

Isn't it ironic, Mother? The girl who flinches at the smallest touch, who feels her throat close at the thought of intimacy, is going around advertising her skin? He said I'm shameless, that my education is a waste, that I'm not worth the effort of teaching. He said he'll take me somewhere else, lock me up, and make me into something he can stomach.

So lately, I've been having prisoner's thoughts.

But what are a prisoner's thoughts? Rage? A burning need to lash out, to do something so vile it leaves a mark. Or maybe just resignation, waiting for the end, too tired to fight anymore. I don't know.

Somehow, I feel all of it.

He forbade me to even see Kaya and said that if I can't open my mouth to agree, I should keep it shut. So, Mother, I went mute.

Silence is easier, after all. To nod and smile when required. To play the part of the obedient daughter while rotting and letting all my burning opinions eat me up from the inside. The one hand I thought would always hold me from falling, the one that was supposed to bleed for me, is the one bleeding me dry.

Sometimes, I want to scream. Sometimes, I want to disappear. And sometimes, I just want to do what he asks, become what he wants. Because fighting feels pointless. I'm already hollowed out.

I can't even look at him nowadays because of the dream a few days back. It wasn't real—thank God, it wasn't — but it felt so real. I could be mistaken for a piece of plastic. With all that weight and hurt, all I could feel was numb.

Utterly empty.

I had hoped I would feel better in the morning. I woke up feeling worse, and now I couldn't bear to look at him without feeling like I'm back in it. Something's so terribly wrong with me. He thinks I hate him. I don't hate him. Isn't that the sick part, Mother? I should hate him. I want to hate him. But all I feel is this warped, painful love that sticks to my bones.

Maybe that's what I hate really is—just love gone rotten. To love is so tragic. While hate is just a mask, a love too painful to exist. Hate is maddening, deafening, cutthroat. I hate you because you can handle my hate. But not my love. I love him, because my hate will devour him whole.

I forgave him, Mother. I forgave everyone. If I had held it against them, everything everyone ever did to me, I'd be crushed under the weight of my vindictiveness.

But forgiveness doesn't wipe the slate clean. I can forgive, but I cannot forget. I write to forget, but all I do is remember.

Each memory is a scar. Those scars are mine. They're a part of me now, in my blood, in my breath. Every step I take carries the weight of them. So, I smoke. I write. I pretend. And I wait for a day that feels lighter than every passing one.

22 June 2024

Mother,

Anger. It's such a funny word, isn't it? People throw it around like it's nothing, like it's just a way to seem composed or nonchalant. Especially lately, everyone's been talking about it like it holds no meaning. All the people I'm familiar with say it's something that makes you yell, argue, or makes you say something you shouldn't. It causes discomfort, they say. That's all it is to them. But for me, anger isn't that simple. It's like poison inside me. It spreads through my veins, filling every part of me until I can't breathe. A rope I hang myself with. I feel like I need to claw it out—out of my heart, my brain, from every cell of mine—or else I may never regain my clarity.

Sometimes, it's so overwhelming I feel like gauging my own eyes out, ripping apart my skin, tearing out my flesh until my bones are exposed and seen. Just to get rid of the venom inside of me. Sometimes, I feel like destroying everything around me, everything alive, so for once, they'd feel even a fraction of the pain I carry every single day. And yet, they call it a feeling. Like it's something small, something you can overlook.

I wish it were that easy. But it's suffocating. And it suffocates me. The poison in me has infected my blood.

I get you now, Mama; I do get you, and surprisingly, I forgive you.

You couldn't have pretended forever; neither can I. Maybe the place where you found your peace is the place where I will find mine. Maybe then I'll finally be home. ~~Maybe I'll final see you.~~

I pray to God, if he exists, that Rayan finds a home as well.

Someone he loves who can love him back.

6 July 2024

Samara,

"Is life not a 1000 times too short for us to lose ourselves?"

lone birds loved the way you moved,

they saw them in you.

trapped and scared,

wishing for a moment to live-

where agony is far away from reach,

and you would dance by the beach.

 the ocean's water rhyming along your feet

damping your soles, a soft retreat.

altered with sand that cuts and bleeds-

the blood dripping down your feet

would colour the ocean dark green.

In arid hearts, your absence breeds thorny cacti.

I reach for them, staining my hands with crimson; licking your love off my fingers.

June 29, 2024

Rayan

I feel a pain in my chest so raw it feels like metal splintering beneath my ribs.

It's been two weeks.

Two entire weeks since I last saw her.

Two weeks crippling me with anxiety and worry, gnawing at me with a hunger that feels like it's eating my soul.

Every other day wasn't enough for me—how could I possibly be okay with this perpetual silence, this absence?

My soul obsesses over her, screams to possess every piece of her, to hold her pain and make it mine, to bleed with her if it meant she wouldn't have to be alone.

That day, when she saw her father, it was like the light had drained from her entirely. Her eyes were vacant, empty in a way that terrifies me.

Her father's eyes lacked emotion and looked so relentless under that calm façade, I wanted to tear through it, to shield her from it, to pull her away from the weight he cast on her shoulders.

But she didn't look back. I knew then that she didn't want me to follow, but I waited.

Every day, I waited for her to return. But she didn't. And this agony has been swallowing me whole.

I've called her, over and over, and the silence on the other end has been deafening.

Yesterday, out of sheer desperation, I texted her that she needed to see me today, or I'd show up at her door uninvited.

I couldn't keep this torment in check any longer. I just needed to see her. To know she's still here. And she's okay.

She replied to that. She told me she wasn't well but when I insisted, she said I could meet her on her apartment terrace for a short while.

So here I am.

The terrace is a vast space, the edges low, three sides lined with glass, the fourth wall reaching my chest. Potted flowers cover most of the area.

I hear footsteps behind me. My heart pounds as I turn. Relief washes over me—but it's brief, immediately shadowed by despair as my heart visibly falters.

Her eyes widen a bit when she sees me. Her hand lifts instinctively, fingers brushing my cheek as if she's unsure I'm real.

Then she pulls back.

I stand frozen. She's here, but why do I feel like I've already lost her?

Her skin is pale, her face bare, flushed without makeup.

Her hair fights the wind, but it's the coral colour of her eyes. God, her eyes seem to be brimming with a pain so vast it could rip the sky apart. I feel it creeping into me.

I step forward, slowly, and wrap my arms around her, pulling her into me. She doesn't resist. She doesn't move. Her frail arms ghost around me, barely there. Her head rests against my chest, and her skin burns like fever. She smells like rain on blazing earth and feels like my own ruin.

Then she trembles.

And trembles.

It starts small, then grows until she's breaking apart in my arms.

My chest caves in. I feel myself unravelling, as though her pain is bleeding into me, making me weaker.

I should ask her what's wrong.

I should demand to know.

But the words die in my throat. I want to destroy whatever's hurting her. But I also want to stay, hold her through this.

I tighten my grip, but she feels like smoke in my hands, like she could disappear if I blink.

She lifts her face, and the desolation in her eyes makes me want to scream. I gently cup her face, pushing back the strands of hair sticking to her damp skin. I'm so close I can see the faint freckles on her cheeks, so close I can feel her breath trembling against mine.

I don't know her.

Not fully.

But I love her.

Every hidden part of her.

Her voice is barely a whisper when she speaks. "Rayan, what are we even doing?"

I search for words that don't exist. What are we doing? I don't know. But this feels real. This feels like falling and flying all at once.

"I don't know," I breathe. "But I know I want to stay. I know I want to fight for you."

Her breath hitches. "Please leave."

I can't. I won't. Not like this. She's pushing me away. Again.

My eyes catch something red beneath the edge of her long sleeves. I reach for her arm.

She jerks back, but my hold is firm. "Please, Rayan. Just leave me!"

My fingers trace the angry welts on her skin, stretching the length of her arm. Slowly, I turn her wrist over-scars. The skin is cut down and tormented. My blood turns to ice. Why didn't I see this before?

"That's why it's always your left hand?" My voice is hoarse. "That's why it's full sleeves and bracelets? Did you do this, or did he? Samara, answer me!"

Her head shakes violently. "It's none of your business. No one did anything to me!"

"This is abuse. Samara, please—what happened?" My voice fractures. Give me something, Samara.

I need to do something. Anything. She's legally of age. My mother can help. There has to be a way out for her.

Her eyes glisten, pleading. "Please leave. Nothing happened."

"I love you, my love. It's killing me to see you like this, let alone leave."

Her face crumbles further. She stumbles away, clutching her stomach like she can't breathe. She sinks onto the platform to the side, tears streaking down her face.

I kneel in front of her. Her hand trembles as it touches my face.

"It'll be better," I whisper.

She shakes her head, whispering, "Rayan, others' perspective of 'better' has always been my misery. You can't fix this. You can't fix me."

I want to argue, to scream, to tell her she's wrong. But the words choke in my throat because she's not entirely wrong.

I can't erase the past or undo the scars etched into her skin and her soul.

But that doesn't mean I won't try. I won't stop trying.

What I can do is take the pain from her present.

Her hand drops from my face to her lap, and I take it gently, wrapping my fingers around hers. She doesn't pull away this time, and it feels like the smallest victory in a war I refuse to lose.

"It's not about fixing you, Samara," I murmur. "You are flawless to me, the way you are. And I just want to be there for you."

I love her the way she is.

Her eyes darken with disbelief. She shakes her head,

"You don't understand," she whispers, her voice breaking. "You'll leave. Everyone leaves.

Love .... Love is nothing but an eternal delusion."

"No. I won't. I don't care how many times you push me away, or how much you try to convince me you're better off alone. I'm not going anywhere."

Her tears fall faster now, carving rivers down her cheeks. I feel like my lungs are filling with stones.

The summer heat scorches through her, as if setting fire to the last traces of hope within.

I reach up, brushing them away with my thumb, my hand cradling her face. She leans into my touch.

"It'll be better," I whisper again, softer this time.

She closes her eyes, her head tilting forward until it rests against mine.

"Stay. Just for a while.", her eyes plead.

"I promised" I breathe, and I mean it. For as long as she'll let me, I'll stay. Even if she doesn't, I would.

I am not leaving her like this. I'll make sure she lives the life she deserves.

7 July 2024

Samara,

"We should consider every day lost on which we have not danced at least once."

You know, they say a kiss could destroy a philosophy. I wonder if that's true. It might be. But do you think I'd agree with it?

No.

Not until I have experienced it on my own.

The lips I crave would never touch mine and wrap their warmth around me. Instead, they'd tremble in fear of being consumed by me. And perhaps that's fair because I would consume them.

But if, just once, those lips—those that have haunted me—finally touched my skin... Do you think I'd hold back?

No.

I would let go of everything I ever was and am, to make that moment my whole existence. My entire being dissolves into it like salt in ocean water.

As they say,

" *By you I am forever undone*"

June 29, 2024

Samara

In the race of running away from the very things that haunted me, the things I despised, I've come to the unsettling realization that I've been running straight toward them. After years of fighting it, I've learned that denial only pushes me deeper into the abyss.

I can keep lying to myself, telling the same story time and time again—that this is what survival demanded, that I had no choice but to be this way. But that's not true. Perhaps I am who I am because it was easier. I don't like the person I've become, but I find some odd ease in the veil I wear every time I look at my reflection.

I'm an orphan to any morals I was taught and now live by my own rules, my sense of right and wrong.

There are times when my vision blurs, and I can't see the guilt. But I can see my soul—cleft like glass but somehow still appealing. Sharp enough to cut, lethal if close enough.

And yet, knowing what I am, alive and aware, people still lean in, blinded by arrogance, critically close to harm, convinced they can control it. If they get hurt, am I truly to blame for that?

What is hurt if not a remainder of love's abandoned sanctuary?

I love him.

The tragedy isn't that I love him.

It's that I can't.

I shouldn't.

This love is a poison I can't spit out and I keep drinking it, craving it, knowing it's killing me.

My room feels like my grave. I collapse to the floor, my knees hitting the ground hard.

My hands claw at my skin, raking over old scars and fresh wounds.

I dig in, deeper and deeper, desperate to peel away this decaying skin.

The way I left him standing there, his eyes soaked with love and fear, guts me. He's the one who needs to breathe. To exist beyond this black hole, I've become.

Not me.

I've been on borrowed air for years. Even if I die, I'll be carrying my casket.

I reach for my journal.

My trembling hands flip through its pages– filled with words and charcoal that kept me alive all these years.

But tonight, they betray me.

The pen shakes in my grip, the words refuse to come out.

The pages drink my tears– blot by blot–until the ink runs wild, bleeding across the paper like my open wounds.

It's *all falling apart.*

I reach for the blade.

My hand moves on its own.

The skin splits open, and the blood pools red, smearing against the pale flesh of my wrist. I chastise, chastise myself for loving my parents.

Chastise myself for not loving myself enough.

For not being enough.

But even this doesn't bring me relief. I watch my blood spill numbly, as if it belongs to someone else. I feel no pain.

It's *maddening*.

I'm losing the control I spent my life mastering.

God, I love him. But I can't let him love me back.

He's my oblivion and I'm his lost sanity. I can't drag him into this abyss. My love won't let me ruin him. I cannot let my torment swallow him whole.

The thought of losing him asphyxiates me.

This is what I feared.

He's a scar stitched into my bones. No matter how much I bleed, I can't cut him out.

He thinks I'm the moon, but I am drained of all my light, and I can only introduce him to the dead of the night.

I wrap my wrist in a cloth, watching it stain red.

I change into a flannel to hide the cuts and swallow aspirins ... one.. two...three..

I lose count - a pathetic attempt to mute the thoughts. I'd rather be numb than give in to my feelings.

It's suffocating.

This mind of mine has reached its anticipated death.

June 29, 2024

Samara

I take the lift ten floors down. My hands are trembling, my vision blurry, as I press the doorbell to Kaya's flat.

I don't trust myself right now. There's too much inside me, I can't hold in anymore.

I just need to talk to someone. Plus, my head hurts and the bleeding just won't stopp.

I ring again, my pulse bashing against my skull.

An older, petite woman opens the door. I blink at her in confusion.

"Can I help you?" Her tone is cautious as she takes me in.

I swallow hard.

"I – I'm looking for Kaya. Who are you?"

The woman frowns.

"I think you have the wrong flat. There's no Kaya here."

I check the flat number.

This is it.

Why is this woman lying?

"She lives here. This is her flat." My voice wavers, but my tone is assertive. Another tear slips down my cheek.

"Honey, I don't know who you're talking about," she says, with a hint of irritation.

"You must be mistaken."

Then she shuts the door in my face.

The world tilts.

Did... did Kaya leave? Did something happen?

I fumble for my phone, my fingers shaking, searching for her contact. My breath catches.

She's not there.

There's no contact.

I type her name again. Nothing. I check my messages. No history.

No. No, this isn't right.

I searched for her on social media. There's no account.

I can't breathe. I feel nauseous. My shirt sleeves are soaked, and blood is dripping on the marble.

I turn and run back to my flat. Each second drags like a blade hanging above my head.

The doors open, and I stumble into the flat, the walls closing in on me.

I don't know what to do. This can't be right.

My hands are quivering as I dial my father. He picks up almost instantly.

"Papa–Papa, Kaya–she's not there. She is not at her place. S- She's gone. Did something happen? Did you delete her contact? Where did she go? I don't understand–"

Deafening silence is the answer I receive.

"Papa?"

I hear a loud crash on the other end, something shattering.

His voice is eerily calm as he states,

"She doesn't exist, Samara. There is no Kaya."

The floor beneath me disappears. I feel like I'm free falling.

"What?"

"She. Is. Not. Real."

"No–what are you saying? Papa, what are you saying?", I sob.

"We'll talk when I get home. Take the yellow bottle tablets and try to sleep."

He hangs up.

I stare at the phone in my hand, and the world around me melting.

I crawl, reaching for the drawer, for the meds I've been taking for years. My father said they were vitamins. My nails dig into the label, peeling it at the edges. I scratch at it, struggling to find the name beneath.

Risperidone.

Antipsychotic medication.

I freeze.

I am not my mother.

I'm not mad. I'm not—

No, this is a game.

My mind strains as I try to remember every memory with Kaya.

She's real.

She must be.

I know the way she loves her toasted bread with melted mozzarella,

How she waits just long enough for the cheese to stretch,

But never long enough for it to cool.

I know how she rides her bike- not just what she rides,

But the way her hair dances in tune with the wind while she hums her favourite song.

But what colour was her bike?

Red? No, maybe blue? It must be green.

The harder I think, the more my head aches.

The more I try to reach, the faster she slips.

If she was never real, why does she feel like a whisper in an empty room? A name on the tip of my tongue. A word erased from a story I used to know.

I pull out my phone and open my gallery. Why are there no pictures? Why can't I remember introducing her to anyone?

Why—why—why—

My head feels like someone is drilling through it.

What is real? What the fuck is real?

I reach for my phone again. Rayan.

His name is there. Our messages, our calls. He's real.

I can't be my mother, I can't. I am not.

I want more than just these four suffocating walls, painted with falsehood and shadows of deceit. I won't let them define me, won't let them decide who I am.

I was written into this fate, but I don't want it to be the last thing written about me.

I grab the soaked journal that has been lying on the floor for so long and just at the corner of my eyes. My head hurts. I'm struggling keeping my eyes open. My hands barely move. They're staining everything. All the words that could bleed into love for my father, all the words that could leave us just alright, come out like tears that deserve to be cried away.

Dear father,

I mustn't wait much longer. Disappointment awaits me, she has cleared a space for me in her grand abode. Both her sisters, Misery and Woe, have come to be my own, they hold up beautiful dresses and they ask me if I take a liking to them. Dear father, reach out for a rose once in a while for you will see them in your slumber. Stretch out the hands that bless the version that was entirely made for you. Father, I find the truth to be true for me, but it is bitter for you, I am not her. Failure built me a home from her ribs, and I cannot ignore her anymore. She lives and speaks to me, father. And hence, dear father, I must leave, for they see me for what I truly am, a proud disgrace. Don't illuminate the vanity in me, father, I do not deserve it. She does, the version of me in you. We never had issues, dear father. I never knew your love, and you never knew mine. What's in a blunder but just a heart and a person? Perhaps I should blame myself and this desiccated, decaying mouth that knows not how to praise you. I should blame these limbs, for it knows not how to walk with you. Don't

~~you worry, dear father, you have done everything to me, but for me? Nothing at all.~~

~~Love,~~

~~Samara~~

I cross it all out, my pen digging in and scratching until it tears and continues tearing the rest of the pages apart. The lights in my room start going off, one by one by-

24 June 2024

Savour the red that drips from my hands
Yes, it is my anger, but it also the color of the
Lipstick my mother used to wear
Before beauty forsake her,
Before she married rage
He forsakes her for lady luck
Now everything comes down to either a kiss or a
drop of blood

A bowl of my honey- dipped sacrifices with a
platter of disappointment
Makes a cocktail of my entire existence
And to be fair
I don't even like honey
Who says poetry needs rhyme to exist, mother?
It only needs a pen and a poet
To make nonsense sensible
And to make misery amiable.

Rayan

Everything is covered in a yellowish hue, usually I'd say it's pretty and so would Samara but today it's giving me a headache.

Samara, Samara, Samara.

That's all I've been thinking about. It's been a day since I last saw her. She's back in her shell, avoiding me again, something is pulling her away, and I can feel it, but I don't want to push.

I miss her.

So, this evening, I decided to check, hoping to see her, even if just for a second.

I must see her. Just make sure she's okay.

I take the lift to the terrace and push open the glass door slowly, almost afraid to disrupt her peace.

And there she is.

I catch a glimpse of her just at the edge, her back to me.

The wind moves through her hair, streaks of red along those earthy hues, swaying just as magical as they can. She looks like one of heaven's greatest, most magnificent angels; with her silhouette drawn against the fading shades of the sky. Painting a painting of serenity just by being present.

It's so calm, too calm.

She remains motionless, and I see crimson trailing down her wrists, dripping from her fingertips, hitting the concrete below.

The surrounding scene seems to be from an impressionist piece of art.

I feel my throat clench in a sad attempt to call out to her, to scream her name, call her to me, but nothing comes out. I am frozen because it is too hard for me to comprehend the sight in front of me.

My eyes burn and a breath catches—stuck between my lungs and my powerlessness.

Just like I had wished earlier, I see her for a second. Before I can do something. Before I can even move a muscle, in the blink of an eye, she is gone.

- Forever and forevermore.

Till death do us apart-

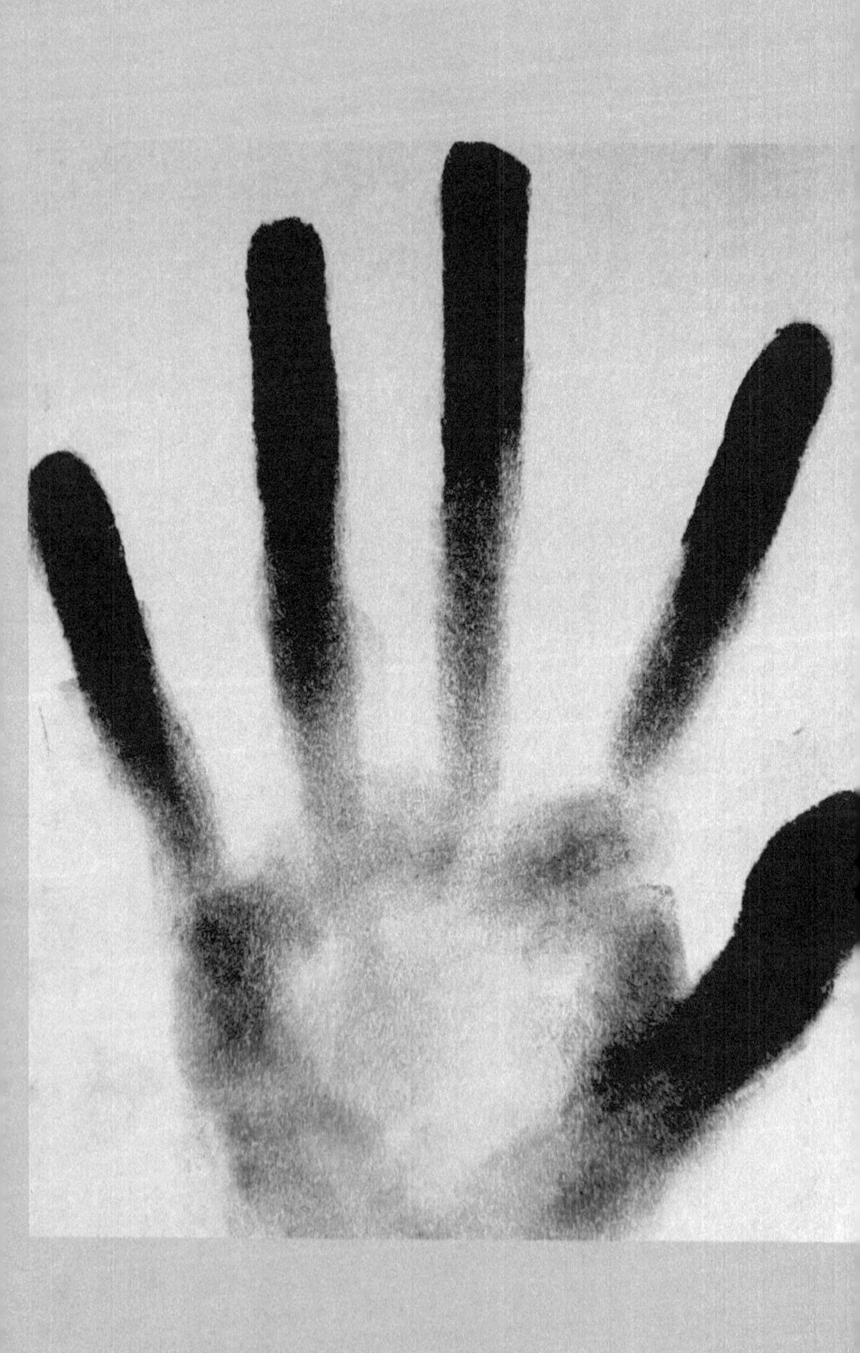

June 30, 2024

Rayan

Various sounds surround me, people begging for miracles, screams of pure desperation, happy tears but what drowns this place is misery.

My hands are buried in my face as I sit in the waiting room outside the ER. The walls feel like they're closing in on me.

My fists clench at my sides, knuckles white, my veins thrumming with anger, guilt, and helplessness. I need to hit something.

Someone.

I need to burn the entire world to the ground.

I should have known.

I shouldn't have left her.

My ribs feel like they'd collapse under the weight of what I didn't do. I feel like I've been crushed into nothing.

Yesterday.... yesterday—I saw it in her eyes, the way she looked past me, the emptiness in her gaze.

I could see something pulling her away from me. God, I didn't want to push.

She's already buried deep, and the last thing I want is to be another weight dragging her down. Even if she doesn't love me back—even though every part of me knows she does—I can't force her hand.

So, I let her be.

I gave her space.

And now I'm here, in this hell, paying for that mistake.

I told my mother everything, not caring about pride or secrecy anymore, I begged her for help. She promised to speak to the prosecutor, to find some way to tear Samara out of the long-suffering propriety she's been caught in.

I'd tear down the entire system if I had to.

She promised she'd call. And like a fool, I trusted her. I waited all night for her voice, but the phone never lit up. I called her after midnight—once, twice, a hundred times, until morning—and she didn't answer.

My stomach churned with dread. I couldn't sleep, I was restless, my mind racing through every possibility, every reason why. And worse, there was no other contact I had with her.

At some point, exhaustion got the better of me, and my eyes closed for long enough for the nightmare to take hold. It was gut wrenching and paralysed by fear.

I've read "when time weeps the presence of the present it leaves you with dread, utterly profound and sinful sense of dread", I think this was it.

I made up my mind to check up on her. I went to her apartment, but nobody answered.

In vain, I tried one last time—one last call. This time, someone picked up.

Her father.

My heart stopped. I knew something was wrong.

He found her late at night. In a pool of blood. Her wrists were tormented and her body lifeless.

My head spun as the world shattered.

My vision blurred with rage and fear, my ears ringing.

They've been trying to stabilize her.

Trying.

Six hours now, and all I can do is sit here, useless, as they fight to pull her back from the brink.

My eyes burn, my hands shake. God, if you're listening—if you're there—please, I'm begging you. Save her. Bring her back to me.

The door to the ER opens, and her father steps out.

His face, marked with guilt and fear, sends my blood boiling. Blind rage fills me as I rise, and before I can think, my fist collides with his face. He stumbles back, but I'm not done. I hit him again, harder this time, but then I stop myself.

This is her father, Rayan.

I force myself to step back, my chest heaving, my hands trembling. He doesn't fight back. He doesn't say a word.

His eyes, bloodshot, drop to the floor. In shame, He's sorry now? His pathetic remorse won't save her. Nothing can undo what he's done.

He walks up to me, his hand heavy on my shoulder.

"She's in a coma."

Three days.

It's been three days since I've heard her voice, three days since I've seen her smile.

I miss her so much, it hurts.

I sit beside her bed, her pale hand limp in mine. My lips press to her fingers, willing her to wake, to move, to just give me something.

Anything.

Her father let me stay when he realized I wasn't going to leave.

My mother came yesterday, concern etched across her face. She asked me about the case, about the next steps, but I told her to wait.

This decision is Samara's. It must be hers. I won't let her go back to that life, but I won't take away her agency either.

My father's eyes held pity, as though he thought I was holding on to a false hope. But it's not false. She'll wake up. I know she will.

I've seen distance in her eyes before, moments where she looked like she didn't want to live. But never, not once, have I seen the will to die. Not in her.

She told her mother she wanted to live. I believe her. I believe in her.

- -

The first night, her father approached me again.

He looked distorted, his grief had moulded him into something unrecognizable. He handed me a bottle of water and asked if I'd eaten. I didn't respond. I couldn't trust myself to speak without letting my fists do the talking.

He sat down next to me and then he told me briefly about Samara's condition. And her mother's, with tears streaming down his face.

It was that night, I realized, the loss of one thing can hold so much power over you, that the successes of life become nothing.

When you lose something valuable, you lose the desire to possess anything ever again.

Then he handed me a diary.

My stomach dropped as I noticed the faint imprint of a hand on the dark cover, like someone had clutched it with bloodied fingers.

I shouldn't have opened it. I knew that much. But my hands moved on their own, trembling as I flipped it open.

The first page stopped me cold.

A drawing—a little caricature of two figures—a little girl holding hands with a larger figure, surrounded by abstract colours. Beneath it, in her familiar distorted cursive: *Samara's.*

My throat tightened. I turned the page, then another, and another.

It wasn't a diary in the traditional sense. It was a collection of letters, sketches, and poems. Words spilled out in jagged handwriting.

I read every word.

Her grief was a living, breathing thing, giving life to every line, every letter. Hers was a sky drowning in ink.

I didn't know it was possible to feel so much sorrow through someone else's words. I didn't know mere words had the power to inflict the pain of a knife stabbing you so deep you feel helpless.

I read until I reached an entry for myself. I read until I reached an entry for her father and then I reached the torn-out pages.

The last two pages, however, were stuck together, the top edge left unsealed.

I slid my fingers into the opening and pulled out what was inside.

Star jasmines.

My vision blurred. My chest heaved with a sob I couldn't hold back.

I cried that day.

For her misery. For her illusions.

She was so terrified of losing everything that she hadn't realized she was losing herself in the process.

She doesn't just need saving.

She needs someone to hold her hand and remind her that she doesn't have to be alone anymore.

When one gives CPR, the breaking of ribs is inconsequential—what matters is the heart. Bones will mend in time, but a lifeless soul cannot be called back.

So, I will wait.

Wait for her to breathe again, to return to herself. And when she does, I'll be there with her as she heals.

Last night, I wrote my entry in her diary, addressed to her.

I read it to her yesterday. I'll read another one to her again today.

And tomorrow, and the day after, for as long as it takes.

"I'm with you, Samara. Even in your sleep.

Like I promised.

Always."

8 July 2024

Samara,

"What is done out of love always takes place beyond good and evil."

Fires are so consuming in sight, aren't they? Watch too closely, and there shall also come a day when the flames consume you whole, without ever touching you.

To pass through the void of your absence, I wrote for you. I wrote to you. For someday I know you'd read these.

Plato once wrote about the soul splitting in two, forever searching for its other half. I don't think we were decent halves of anything.

I think we were broken pieces of glass, drawn together not to complete each other, but perhaps to cut one another even deeper.

28 June 2024

Every fool for every folly
Every poet for every rose garden grandeur
Every folklore for every hopeless romantic
Lullaby for every child
Glance over every apathy that lies

Despair for each and every faith
Forsakes me for a life
Sky, for every time I shed all my
Precedence for a crime

I lost myself every time I wasn't found
I sinned when on finding I wasn't born an angel
I look beautiful because I'm carved of pain
I'm a woman, because of my bleeding veins
I'm pushed to my knees, because I refuse to bow
I'm a daughter because I am lost in faith.

July 9, 2024

Samara

The room feels cold despite the blanket draped over me.

The sterile scent of antiseptic fills my nostrils, the rhythmic beeping of a machine somewhere nearby, humming in my ears.

Everything feels too bright, my eyes hurt. I think I'm dreaming.

I blink, staring up at the ceiling.

What is happening? My head hurts.

A nurse asks me if I'm fine and I nod. Several people in white coats ask me trivial questions. They leave me alone after what seems like hours.

I glance down at my hands.

Bandaged and limp, they look smaller than I remember. Moving them takes too much effort, so I let them rest against the stiff hospital sheets.

The weight of everything crashes down.

What happened?

The memories are fragmented. The blood, the pills. **Kaya**.

A tear slips down my cheek before I even notice. Then another. And another. My chest is trembling with sobs.

I hear voices outside the door. Footsteps of someone coming.

The door creaks open, and I see my father.

He looks older, and so much thinner, as if these past few days have aged him years. His eyes are bloodshot, shoulders slump like the weight of the world has fallen on him.

He takes hesitant steps toward me, stopping just short of the bed. For the first time in my life, he looks... afraid.

His hand trembles as he holds up a piece of archaic folded paper and hands it to me.

I seize breathing. Is this? My heart sinks, something doesn't feel right. His voice reaches me. "I'm sorry for not giving this to you earlier. I'm sorry. That..tha- day, I found this in the gun's place."

Tears spill without my say. I cannot open it. He kept it from me all these years.

"Samara," he mutters, his voice cracking. He looks horrified.

I don't say anything. I don't know what to say. I just listen.

He kneels beside me, his head bowed like he can't bear to meet my eyes. When he continues, his voice is so broken, I question reality once again.

"I loved her."

My heart clenches.

"I loved Sarah," he breathes, his voice stuttering. "Your mother....I- I loved her more than anything. More than myself. And when she..." He chokes, his hand trembling as he reaches for mine.

I pull back instinctively, and he freezes, his head bowing in shame.

"When she died, I couldn't accept it. I lost her, and I thought I'd lost everything."

He looks at me then, really looks at me, and his eyes filled with something I've never seen before: regret.

"And you," he continues, his voice breaking.

"You looked so much like her. I loved you..I loved you with everything I had. The first time you told me you had a friend when you were 3, I did a background check because I was concerned, only to find out it was all in your head. You had made her up.

I was heartbroken. I didn't know what to do. Every time I looked at you, it was like seeing her all over again. It hurt. It hurt so much that I—" He stops.

"I know that doesn't excuse anything. I know I hurt you. Hurt you in ways I can never take back. But Samara... that night..." His voice cracks further. "When I found you like that... I thought I'd lost you, too."

Tears stream down his face. He's sobbing. My father. He looks like a man who's being crushed under the weight of his sins.

"I don't deserve your forgiveness," he struggles to get the words out. "I know that. But please, Samara. Don't do this again. Please. You're my daughter. You are our miracle. And I... I can't lose you. I'll go to therapy and I...I accept if you want to stay away from me...or report me ... I just can't lose you."

For a long moment, I just stare at him, my face slick with teras, trying to process his words. For a moment, I even think I'm dreaming, that this is not real.

But it is.

For so long, he's been this unfeeling figure with no regard for my feelings. Now he's kneeling in front of me, begging for something I'm not sure I can give.

From what I know from my aunt, my mother and father were high school sweethearts. She was diagnosed with schizophrenia.

He knew.

Loved her anyway.

Loved her past reason.

Past help. So much he made her stop her medication because it dulled her–made her a ghost. Things were good for a while. Then they weren't. When she got pregnant with me, she tried to end herself, multiple times. She started her medication again after that. She spent months under watch. But after I was born, it got worse. Seven months later, while my father was away, she...shot herself.

Maybe my mother and I are more alike than I thought. I came from her after all.

"It wasn't your fault," I whisper finally. His head snaps up, a sparkle of hope in his tired eyes.

No, it is not his fault my mother died. I know that. She was suffering beyond reason.

And I have seen him suffer for her death, as if he blames himself. He shouldn't.

"It wasn't your fault that Mom died," I repeat, my voice firmer this time.

"*And you won't be the reason I do,*" I add.

His face crumples, and for the first time in years, I see him for what he is: just a man.

He is flawed. He is hurt. He is human.

It doesn't make what he did okay. It doesn't erase the years of pain. But it's a start.

And at the end of it all, he is my father. No matter how much I try to hate him, I never truly can.

There are people in this world who would trade anything for even a little percentage of what he gave me. And I know too well that most who suffer with mental illness are cast out.

So I'll give him a chance—not because he deserves it, but because maybe we both do not. He needs healing. He needs therapy. And for the first time, I can admit it—so do I.

He rises slowly after a while, wiping his face with shaking hands. "I wish I could be there for you the way he was- if not more," he says, before stepping out of the room.

I don't have to ask who he means.

Rayan.

When he walks in, my heart is once again filled with dread.

He looks exhausted–dark circles under his eyes, his face pale, his body slouched with weariness. But the moment he sees me; it's like something in him comes back to life. *Oh god.*

He rushes to my side, his hands trembling as they hover over mine, unsure if he should touch me.

"Rayan," I whisper. A tear escapes my eye, rolling down my cheek.

His eyes flood with relief as he leans closer, his warmth filling the space between us. I reach out, my hand brushing his, needing to know he's real.

He's real. He's here.

He leans down and presses his forehead to mine, his voice a soft murmur.

"I'm here, Samara, as long as you'd want me to."

This time, I believe him.

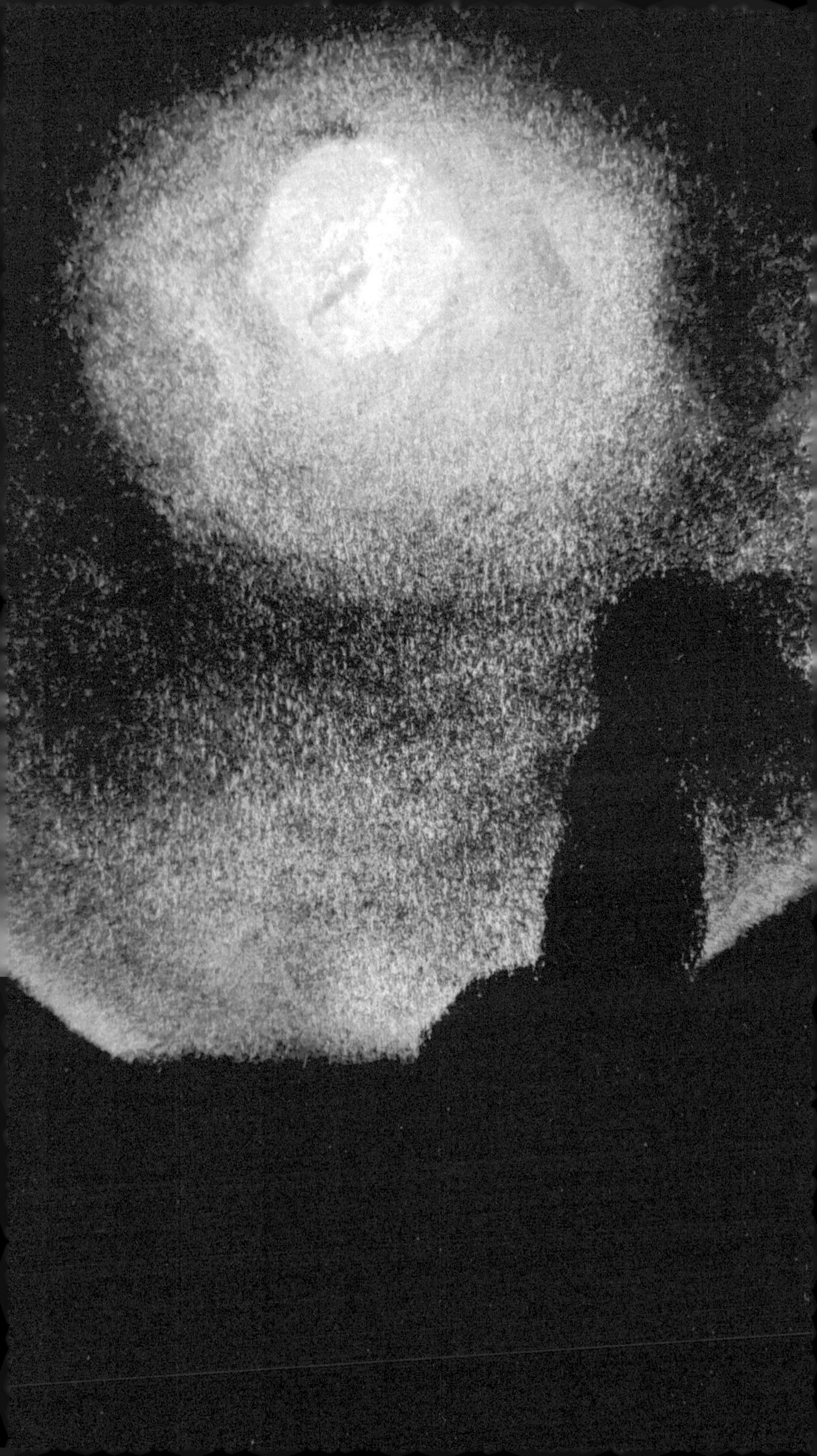

February 13, 2003

Samara,

My baby,
You know, I am 25 today—and 21 days.
I am also 84 today.
And, at the same time, I am 10 days old too.
You ask me why?
I'll tell you why.

I am 25 because I can't cry in public. I must carry everything inside me. I am a wife, a mother,
A daughter.
21, for the 21 good days of my life.
They include the days your father and I spent together, and the day you were born.

84 years, for the experiences that have shaped me, the shroud of shame that covers me and darkness that seems to swallow me.

10 days, for the helplessness of a child I still carry within.

I don't have dreams—not anymore.

Perhaps I did, once.

I dreamt of things so vast, so consuming,

And in the worst joke played by God ever,

The dreams came true and swallowed my ability to sleep.

And yes, I got what I wanted—

 I'm just not sure if it's a victory,

Or a loss my heart can't recover from.

But you know what victory was for me?

It was when I gave birth and I looked into my own eyes, to find innocence

And so much light.

I touched your skin, and it felt sacred.

That's when I knew I was blessed and that's when I knew I couldn't tarnish it.

That's when I swore, I will protect you,

From me.

Open your heart to all the love you get and be kind, my baby.

You are a daydream, my daydream,

 my miracle.

I love you.

I hope you grow up to be anything and everything you want.

Just nothing like me.

Love, mama.

Epilogue

August 3, 2024

Hey. I was thinki—

She pressed a kiss to his cheek. Soft, subtle, gentle, polite.

He was momentarily stunned. She looked at him and beamed with such radiance that he felt as though a thousand stars had fallen, leaving only one behind—his brightest star.

His Samara.

She carried a child-like happiness, an innocence that seemed to surround her entire being.

And yet, in that moment, he thought: how could someone who had endured so much exude such strength?

He was falling in love.

With her strength.

With her ability to live, despite it all.

With the way she helped him rediscover himself and reminded him that love, in the end, sustains everything.

That love is all there was, all there is, and all there ever could be.

He had built these walls around himself, and somehow, she had managed to slip through the smallest of cracks, and seep in all those hollow parts of him that were left void.

Her presence managed to fulfil every single deserted island, every crater of his being, with something so majestic, he'd call her a miracle if she'd let him.

He had been lost in thought for so long that she had to poke him to get his attention.

How beautiful it was to hold on to someone in your thoughts and, when you return to the world, find them standing right in front of you.

"My eyes wouldn't see anyone if it weren't for you, Samara," he said.

She blushed, and as he leaned closer, he whispered, "May I?"

She smiled.

He kissed her eyelids.

And somehow, in that simple touch, it was as if every wound she had ever seen through those eyes was soothed. The torn fragments of her past seemed to stitch themselves together.

Human touch was miraculous.

Love—maybe it was the miracle.

She didn't know for sure. All she knew was that she had been torn apart, and now she was being pieced back together.

Maybe, she thought, she could be an endless cloth, one he would weave for eternity. She wouldn't mind at all.

In fact, she would welcome it.

She sighed and rested her head against his chest.

Warmth.

The hard, worn cloth was being handled with gentle hands.

The cloth was willing to change–its perspective, its texture–because the hands were kind.

Because he was so gentle as he held her and sniffed her hair.

She could go on like this forever.

She would never tire of this. Of him. Of his scent.

He reached into his pocket then, pulling out something -a bracelet.

Gold, thin. It was like the one she gave him. He clasped it around her wrist with such care, as if it were a crown.

Her fingers traced the bracelet, she looked up at him, her voice barely a whisper. "I love you."

For a second, she thought he might not have heard her. But then his lips curved into the softest smile, and he leaned in, pressing a kiss to her forehead.

"I love you, Samara."

He was just grateful for her red, her love. The love that consumed his heart whole eventually and set it on fire.

Or was his heart ashen long before the realization of it all hit? She would be the death of him.

But he wouldn't mind being buried in her love at all.

In her eyes, the world was an illusion. In his, she was the world.

Editor's Notes'

IT WAS ALL US

Did you do it on purpose or was it a lie?

You're so different,

I lie to myself to see you as alive

When he hung himself, did you die too?

While he went to motels

A beginning wasn't there to begin when it
comes to us

So busy being a good person,

you sacrificed us in the process

I can't even imagine being in your shoes

Whether it's stripped childhood or calamity in
the walls of your own home,

I tip toed around my life trying to not make a
sound

So why do I end up in the middle of
the feud?

Don't you realise the two blades always
seemed to cut me through

Now I can't love someone even if I
wanted to

what did I do to deserve the hell you
gave me

Pretended everything is normal while bureing
me illicitly

But it's getting hard to breathe now

I wanna shove you in the same grave you
buried me

-Arpita Singh

the ones always looked upon

were beholders of divine beauty.

now the question awakening my sleeping
heart-

how much of thy soul was seen?

it was rather, fettered by their own beauty,

and while thou didst beg to be seen,

thou wert looked at.

never to be seen, slept upon thy beauty.

'Twas always thus,

Always thus shall be.

- Elyvia Sttilwright.

Acknowledgments

In my nineteen years of existing (often dramatically), I extend my deepest gratitude to the many people who have, at some point, called me insane or tried to bring me down. Your words lost their sting after a while, and, well—look where my delusions have brought me. Take a moment for yourself. I hope you're all living your best lives.

To my wonderful parents—thank you for birthing a hopeless romantic and never hesitating to call me out on my nonsense. I owe you for keeping me somewhat grounded.

To *The Beatles* and *Muse*—on behalf of all of us, thank you for creating such soul-crushing music. This book would not have come to life without my incredible proofreaders—Kavya, Anisha and Mysha, you are the real MVPs. Arpita, your endless suggestions saved me. Aman, you gave CPR to my vision with your creativity, I owe you my dreams since you quite literally designed the cover from them and, Arham, thank you for helping me curate an immaculate playlist, with your endless song recommendations giving a soundtrack to each chapter. Kritika, your words of appreciation and artistic skills are absolute magic.

Abaan, Samiya, Ridhima—thank you for believing in me, even though I suspect you all might have unresolved *Justin Bieber* issues.

Most of all, I thank God for blessing me with the specimen of a woman-Riddhima—thank you for being the wolf to my house stark. I genuinely don't think I could've made it here without you.

And of course, my sweetest sugar plums—you, the readers. Thank you for stepping into this world with me. You are the reason these words exist. I adore you endearingly.